"Do you think something bad will happen if I move you?"

Yes.

"Will somebody attack us? Like there's somebody nearby lying in wait?"

No.

"How about a booby trap?"

Yes. Her eyes cut to the floorboards hoping he'd understand.

"Underneath you? Like a pressure-sensitive device?"

Yes! She nodded her head.

"Well, then, I get why you're so twitchy." He set the gun down, reached into his back pocket and pulled out his knife. "It looks like you can move your head freely without setting it off. So now that I know what's going on, I'm thinking that if I'm really slow and careful I can probably cut off your gag and then you can tell me exactly what we're dealing with, okay?"

Yes, but–

She took a breath and then nodded.

"Okay," he said. "Let's do this."

Maggie K. Black is an award-winning journalist and romantic suspense author with an insatiable love of traveling the world. She has lived in the American South, Europe and the Middle East. She now makes her home in Canada with her history teacher husband, their two beautiful girls and a small but mighty dog. Maggie enjoys connecting with her readers at maggiekblack.com.

Books by Maggie K. Black

Love Inspired Suspense

True North Bodyguards

Kidnapped at Christmas

Killer Assignment
Deadline
Silent Hunter
Headline: Murder
Christmas Blackout
Tactical Rescue

Visit the Author Profile page at Harlequin.com.

KIDNAPPED AT CHRISTMAS

MAGGIE K. BLACK

HARLEQUIN® LOVE INSPIRED® SUSPENSE

Recycling programs
for this product may
not exist in your area.

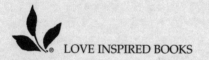

LOVE INSPIRED BOOKS

ISBN-13: 978-0-373-67783-2

Kidnapped at Christmas

Copyright © 2016 by Mags Storey

All rights reserved. Except for use in any review, the reproduction
or utilization of this work in whole or in part in any form by any
electronic, mechanical or other means, now known or hereinafter
invented, including xerography, photocopying and recording, or in
any information storage or retrieval system, is forbidden without
the written permission of the editorial office, Love Inspired Books,
195 Broadway, New York, NY 10007 U.S.A.

This is a work of fiction. Names, characters, places and incidents are
either the product of the author's imagination or are used fictitiously, and
any resemblance to actual persons, living or dead, business establishments,
events or locales is entirely coincidental.

This edition published by arrangement with Love Inspired Books.

® and TM are trademarks of Love Inspired Books, used under license.
Trademarks indicated with ® are registered in the United States Patent
and Trademark Office, the Canadian Intellectual Property Office and in
other countries.

www.Harlequin.com

Printed in U.S.A.

Say to those with fearful hearts,
"Be strong, do not fear; your God will come."
—*Isaiah* 35:4a

Thanks to Roz for giving me a safe place to hide and write.
Thanks to Sunny for the puzzle-piece metaphor.
You are remarkable women, and you both inspire me.

Also, thank you, Bethany, for lending me
your very special headphones when mine broke,
so that I didn't have to write the suspenseful kidnap scene
while listening to "Under the Mango Tree."
You are very awesome and I love you.

ONE

A fierce, biting cold that seemed to dig right into her skin was the first thing journalist Samantha Colt felt as her groggy brain swam back into consciousness.

The second was the sharp tip of the knife pressed against her throat.

"Don't move." The voice was coarse, male and contained more than a hint of a threat.

She froze. She was lying on her back and couldn't move her arms or legs. The metal floor of some kind of vehicle vibrated beneath her. The shriek of December wind rose above the rough sound of the engine. A gag filled her mouth. She opened her eyes and saw nothing but a blindfold.

I've been kidnapped.

The thought hit her like a jolt. But who'd kidnapped her? How had they grabbed her? What could they possibly want?

She had no idea.

Help me, Lord! she prayed.

She closed her eyes again and struggled to piece together the strands of what she could remember. It had been quarter after five in the morning when she'd left her small one-bedroom apartment on the top floor of a converted house in downtown Toronto. There'd been new flyers plastering the staircases. Bright blue this time, with dire warnings from her landlady Yvonne about the dangers of both trespassers and raccoons. The streets were dark. The world was frozen. She'd slipped through the icy back alleys toward the *Torchlight News* office. She'd buried her hands in the pockets of her vintage wool overcoat, feeling for her gloves before realizing she'd left them behind. *And then?*

She wasn't wearing her coat now.

How long ago was I kidnapped? Did I even make it to work?

With Christmas only two days away, the newspaper's office was already closed for the holidays. But she was the newspaper's main fact-checker. She was never really off. Last night her laptop had refused to load, so she'd headed into the office this morning to grab a backup tablet so that she'd have something to work on—because a good story waited for no one.

Samantha had singlehandedly created and updated the paper's research database—nicknamed ATHENA, because "Aggregated Torchlight Hub for Enforcement and News Analysis" was a mouthful. Not that she ever got the glory. Or wanted it, for that matter. Samantha was a desk jockey. Someone who was quite comfortable working in the shadows, making sure overenthusiastic reporters—and their stories—stayed accurate. It was her job to verify that *Torchlight* got every fact right, to see the bigger picture and to even catch patterns that others might miss.

Was that why I was kidnapped? Because of something I researched?

"I think she's awake." The rough voice yanked her attention back to the freezing van. The stench of stale cigarettes filled her lungs. A man seemed to be crouched in the back of the van beside her. A gloved hand pushed a long strand of honey-blond hair off her cheeks. "Or maybe not. I can't tell. She's still breathing anyway. We almost there?"

"How should I know?" A second voice came from the direction of the driver's seat. Also male, but higher-pitched and with a bit of a whistle. Like a mean stray dog who'd lost some teeth in a street fight. "You think I can see any street signs out here?"

The van hit a bump. Her body bounced against the cold, metal floor.

"Hey! Watch it!" The one that smelled like cigarettes swore. The one that whistled laughed. Neither sounded that much older than their midtwenties. Silence stretched out endless around her again, filled with nothing but the howling wind, the bitter cold and the rumble of the engine.

Fear ran cold through her veins. This had to be a dream. This couldn't really be happening. Years ago, in college, she'd been tormented by night terrors for months after a fellow student had broken into her room in the middle of the night. But even at their worst no nightmare had ever felt as real as this.

Come on! Focus! She could think her way out of this. Her bare hands were bound together at the wrists in front of her by what felt like fabric. Her feet were tied together at the ankles by something thin that rustled as she shifted. The road turned rough beneath them.

Who are these people? What do they want? How did I get in this van? She didn't know. Panic swirled like turpentine inside her mind, wiping her memory clean and filling her throat with bitterness. *Facts.* She had to focus on facts, no matter how small. There'd been a congratulations card in her bag for her editor, Olivia Ash, who'd just had a baby girl. There'd been a shiny new billboard for Eric Gibson's morning radio show on top of the Silver Media building. Would Eric suspect something was wrong when she didn't show up for coffee? She'd met the charming radio host a few months ago, when he was dating her neighbor. The neighbor had moved out and moved on, and suddenly Samantha had found herself being Eric's shoulder to cry on.

Was their Christmas coffee today a date in his mind? Or had it finally sunk in that she really did love her single, quiet, workaholic life and didn't need anything more? It was hard to tell if Eric was interested in her romantically or if he was just trying to be a good friend. Figuring out people had never come as easy to her as sorting out facts.

The vehicle slowed to a stop. She heard the metallic shriek of a van side door sliding open.

"What is this? Is that a light on over there?" The one who smelled like stale cigarettes sounded more than a little irritated. "You told me no that one would be here."

"Well, I didn't really know, now did I? Let's just get it over with."

Hands grabbed her ankles and dragged

her out across the floor. She kicked out hard with both feet at once, catching her abductor in what she hoped was something vital. He swore and let go. The bonds binding her legs snapped free. She fell, landed on the ground beside the van and scrambled to her feet. She ran through the snow, waiting any moment to feel rough hands grab her again. A gunshot shook the air. Wet flakes pelted her head. The air was dark around her. However long she'd been in that van, the sun still hadn't risen yet. She kept going, blind, through trees, over the snowy ground, using nothing but differences of light and shadow to guide her, holding her elbows out in front of her to protect her head, as her bound hands struggled to free her eyes from the fabric covering them.

Then a yellow gleam of light shone ahead, so bright the blindfold shone gold.

She ran toward it. The snow turned to gravel beneath her feet. The comforting smell of wood smoke filled her senses. Her knees hit a step. She pitched forward, landing hard on a staircase. With a desperate yank she pulled the blindfold down from her eyes and looked up at the towering farmhouse. A single light shone down from a window on the second floor. She could hear a dog barking inside. The relentless and determined yapping seemed to fill her heart with hope. A window slid open above her.

"Hey! Hello! Is there somebody out there?" A deep, rich voice filled the air, wafting down from above through the pelting snow. Her dark eyes looked up to the shape of the man standing in the window above her. Light shone from behind him, ringing his tall silhouette. He had broad shoulders and strong arms. Her fingers pulled at the tight gag still binding her mouth, struggling to make sound escape her lips.

Yes! I'm here! She yanked at her gag as it stole her voice from her lips. *Help me! Whoever you are, help me!*

"Hello?" he called again. "Is everything all right?"

Please! I think they're going to kill me.

She stumbled to the front door. Her bound hands fumbled for the doorknob. It was locked. The barking grew louder, with the hint of a snarl.

Then the window shut above her. He was gone.

Please, Lord, she prayed. *Wherever I am, whoever this man is, I need his help. He's my only hope.*

Footsteps sounded heavy and hollow on the wood behind her. She turned and caught a quick glance of an old, ugly scar slashed across an unfamiliar face. Gloved hands shoved her down onto the snow-covered porch. She kicked out hard, twisting her body against the man's grasp. But he held firm. One hand slid something hard and round underneath the small of her back.

She tried to sit up. But he pushed her down. The device beneath her clicked.

"Now listen carefully, Miss Colt," he hissed. The stench of stale smoke filled her nostrils again. He pulled a roll of something red and shiny from his pocket. "There's a live land mine under your back. You hear me? A land mine. An explosive. I'm going to tie your legs again and you're going to lie still. Because, if you move, it will explode and you will die."

The dog was still barking, hurtling its tiny furry body through the upstairs hallway of the Ash family's country house so quickly that even with almost a decade of military service under his belt, Corporal Joshua Rhodes of the Canadian Armed Forces could hardly keep up.

Not that the soldier ever needed much of a kick to sprint into action. A few short days of holiday leave was hardly enough time to readjust his system to the quieter rhythms of civilian life. He'd been lying, already dressed, on top of the sleeping bag he'd slung on the bed in the front room, wrestling with whether or not he wanted to reenlist in the army when his term was up in June, when a gun blast cracked the early-morning air. Surely, nobody would be dumb enough to try deer hunting on his friend's private property, and with a handgun no less. But the feeling of concern that had tapped his attention had grown to a full-fledged warning beat when he'd slid open the window, called out and heard nothing but the muffled sounds of a struggle below and someone trying to open the front door.

Well, God, he prayed, *I don't know what's going on out there, but something's very wrong. Help me know what to do.*

Whatever it was, Joshua was about to face it alone.

The Ash family were staying at their apartment in Toronto for a little while after the birth of their new daughter. Their two other houseguests for the holidays, stepsiblings Alex and Zoe, had left the house over half an hour ago for some hard-core early-morning skiing. He'd have gone with them too, but then that army "re-up" reminder email had arrived asking him to commit several more years of his life to a career he'd never particularly enjoyed. But, he was good at it, and if he kept at it he'd eventually retire with a pension, and as Gramps would say, what kind of man walked away from a good job just because he didn't like it? If growing up in a household of only men had taught him anything it was that solitude was best for thinking. So he'd told his friends to go ahead skiing without him while he wrestled with the choices in his mind. That'd left him alone with Zoe's puppy, Oz, who while plenty loud wasn't much for backup.

Joshua's hand slid to the solid, familiar weight of his .45 on his hip. His watch read ten after seven but pitch-black air still pressed up against the windows. He ran quickly but quietly down the wooden staircase into the first floor kitchen, crossed the floor, then paused. The rattling at the front door had stopped. The dog's barking had subsided to a low, threatening growl that rumbled in the back of the Cairn terrier's throat. Joshua grabbed his leather jacket off a hook, shoved his hands into gloves and his feet into his boots.

Then he threw the back door open and heard a voice.

A muffled cry rose on the wind. So faint,

he could barely hear it, but unmistakable nonetheless. There was a woman out there somewhere in the cold and dark. She was frightened. And in trouble.

The gun was tight in his grip. He stepped outside, pressed his body against the side of the house and crept toward the porch. The friend whose house this was—Daniel Ash— was a bodyguard and private security specialist who'd recently hired Alex and Zoe to join him in the business, as he converted the country property into a safe house and home base for operations. Meanwhile, Daniel's wife, Olivia, was a journalist whose newspaper had a reputation for tenaciously exposing criminals and corruption.

The Ashes weren't strangers to tough situations. Joshua couldn't even begin to guess what kind of trouble might be waiting in the darkness. But as he focused his heart on the faint, terrified sound of the woman's cry as it seemed to rise and fall between the gusts of wind, the idea of leaving her alone in the cold while he waited for backup was unthinkable. Joshua reached the corner of the house.

He saw her. She was lying on the porch lit by the dim light from the upstairs window. Her legs were bound just above the cuff of her high-heeled vintage boots. She was wearing thick black tights, a plaid skirt that stopped at the knees and a long-sleeved sweater, but no jacket. Her hands were gloveless and tied together in front of her. Her body was shaking.

So much was wrong with this picture. If she'd been abducted, then why dump her here? If a kidnapper was going to tie her hands, why not tie them behind her back?

He stepped up onto the porch. The wood creaked under his boots. Her head rose. A whimper slipped from her lips. Joshua took a deep breath and prayed that this wasn't a trap. Then he crossed the porch, knowing he was going to do whatever he could to save her life, whether it was a trap or not.

"Hey." He knelt down beside her. "It's going to be okay. My name's Joshua Rhodes. I'm here to help you."

Her face tilted toward him. Large dark eyes looked into his face, framed with long, full lashes and filled with fear. Something in their depths hit him like a one-two punch to the gut. *She was terrified—and she was beautiful.* Cascades of blond hair spread out around her shaking shoulders. He reached for the gag and froze. A gold velvet ribbon parted her lips. Another larger red ribbon had slipped around her throat from what he could only guess had once been a blindfold. Two other ribbons bound her hands and feet. He sat back on his heels. His heart shuddered in horror and sympathy. *She'd been wrapped up like a Christmas present.*

What kind of evil was this? Who would ever do that to someone?

Never let your eyes get all distracted by the looks of a pretty woman. They'll knock your mind off course, distract you from the job you've got to do, and bring you nothing but trouble and pain. His late grandfather's voice suddenly echoed in the back of his mind. Growing up it was the only kind of answer he'd ever really gotten from the widower to questions of why the family was just him, Gramps and Dad. Joshua slid his arms from his leather coat. "I'm just going to drape this over you while we figure on what's going on here."

But she shook her head furiously like she was even scared of his jacket.

God, please help me. He took a deep breath as he prayed. His eyes rose to the skies above. *What kind of trouble is this woman in? What kind of danger am I getting myself into by helping her?*

TWO

Panic rose in Samantha's chest. She could feel the land mine pressing against the small of her back and had no clue how sensitive the trigger was. But if this strange man suddenly dropped his coat on her or moved even a little, would the explosion kill them both?

Please, God, help me make him understand the danger we're in!

Faint morning light now rose at the horizon, casting the snow and trees around them in long shadows and shades of blue. But she could still barely see Joshua's face.

"So, you don't want my coat?" He said the words slowly, like he'd just been thrown a curve ball and was struggling to make sense of what was happening. He set his coat down on the porch beside her. "It's okay. I promise. I won't hurt you. I'm a corporal in the Canadian army. It's my job to help people."

My heart wants to trust you, soldier. But my mind's telling me not to be naive.

Both of his hands rose slightly. There was a handgun in his grasp. "What if we start by my untying your gag?"

"No." Her head shook. The muffled cry sounded more like *nah* than *no*. She closed her eyes. This was useless. She'd never been that great at knowing how to talk to people even when she'd had a voice. Besides, she could shake her head all she wanted, but that didn't mean he'd actually listen. Just like Eric never seemed to hear her whenever she explained she was actually very happy spending her evenings working at home alone and didn't want him showing up with fast food or a DVD. Maybe Corporal Joshua Rhodes was a better man than most. But even still, eventually he was going to just take matters into his own hands, and pick her up or something, and kill them both.

"Go!" she pleaded through her muffled gag. At least one of them should have the opportunity to getting out of this alive. "Run!"

Tears filled her eyes. It was hopeless. Her *go* sounded like *ga* and she couldn't even make a sound that was anything like *run*.

"Go?" he asked.

Thank You, God! He understood that much at least.

"You want me to just leave you here?" He drew his hands back and looked at her like she was a very difficult problem he needed to solve. "You don't want me to touch you, you don't want me to untie you and you don't want my coat? Instead, you do want me to high-tail it out of here—and that's just not going to happen. Right now, you and I are in this together. So, here's how this is going to work, I'm going to ask questions. You're going to nod yes or shake your head no. That work for you?"

She nodded. *Yes.*

"I get that you don't want me to move you or touch you. Is it because you're injured?"

She shook her head. *No.*

"Do you think something bad will happen if I move you?"

Yes.

"Will somebody will attack us? Like there's somebody nearby lying in wait?"

No.

"How about a booby trap?"

Yes. Her eyes cut to the floorboards hoping he'd understand.

"Underneath you? Like a pressure-sensitive device?"

Yes! She nodded her head.

"Well, then I get why you're so twitchy." He set the gun down, reached into his back pocket and pulled out his knife. "It looks like you can move your head freely without setting it off. So, now that I know what's going on, I'm thinking that if I'm really slow and careful I can probably cut off your gag and then you can tell me exactly what we're dealing with, okay?"

Yes, but—

She swallowed back the thought. Her pulse was racing so quickly she was worried it alone might somehow set the land mine off. She hadn't woken up this morning looking for a crash course in trusting her heart.

But, somehow, Joshua, something inside tells me I can trust you.

She took a breath and then nodded.

"Okay," he said. "Let's do this."

She felt the tip of the blade brush lightly against her jaw. It slid under the gag. He breathed a prayer under his breath and flicked the blade upward. The gag tore free.

"Thank you!" She gasped. Then smiled, just slightly, her face creasing in relief. "I'm Samantha Colt."

"Good to meet you, Samantha." He tapped her fingers lightly, like a substitute for a handshake, and then slipped the gag into his jeans pocket. "Now, how about you tell me what's going on?"

"I don't know." Her voice shook. She could guess it had something to do with something she'd been fact-checking for work. Military operations maybe? Criminal gangs? Missing women? Maybe the illegal weapon trade, considering the use of a land mine? But those were all long shots at best. And she wasn't about to start throwing out wild guesses, especially to a stranger. "Honestly, I don't know what happened, why someone would do this to me, or even where I am."

"Hey, it's okay." He set the knife down too. She had no idea how he was managing to keep his voice so calm and yet she appreciated it. "You're in the Ontario countryside, middle of nowhere really, about an hour and a half north of Toronto, at the home of my friend Daniel. He's a bodyguard with a private security business."

It rang a very faint bell. But she couldn't place why. "I don't know who that is."

"Where's the device?" Joshua asked.

"Under the small of my back. He said it was a land mine and that if I moved it would kill me."

"He?"

"The man who tied me up and left me here. He didn't tell me anything except about the land mine. I didn't see much of his face, just that it was scarred. But he stunk like he smoked six packs a day. He had a partner with missing teeth, by the sound of it. They weren't exactly chatty."

"Did you happen to see what the device looked like?"

"No, but it's round and about the size of a bagel. So, like an antipersonnel mine. Too small to be an antitank mine and definitely too flat be a bounding mine. It clicked."

His jaw dropped. "How do you know so much about mines?"

"I'm a fact-checker. I know a little bit about a whole lot of things."

He nodded slowly, like he was absorbing everything she was telling him. His lips moved in what looked like silent prayer. The wind was picking up, tossing the ends of her hair and ruffling her clothes.

"It'll probably take the police over an hour to get here. Even then they might not be able to disarm the explosive, only detonate it." There was a deeper, stronger timbre to his voice now, like a commanding officer preparing his troops for battle. "So, here's what we are going to do. First, I'm going to, very slowly and very carefully, cut the ribbons holding both your hands and your feet—"

"Ribbons?" She'd been able to tell her abductor had tied her feet with something red. But still a shiver of horror slid down her spine at the thought of someone tying her up like a Christmas present.

"Ribbons," Joshua confirmed. "Now, again, I'm going to cut them off and you're going to help by staying very still and not moving, which might be hard considering your instinct's going to be to stretch."

"Got it. I won't move."

She felt the knife brush along her calves. She stayed as still as she could, but even so she could feel the pressure in her ankles shift the moment he cut them free. Then he moved up to her hands. His fingers held hers gently as the knife sliced. Then the bonds fell away. The digging pain disappeared from her wrists. Gently he slid both of his hands over hers and rubbed warmth and life back into her fingers. She almost whimpered with relief.

"Now," he said, "I'm going to slide my hand underneath your back, nice and slowly, until I feel the land mine. Then, I'm going to hold the detonator down. When I do that, I'm going to shout 'go,' and then I need you to roll down the stairs as fast as you can. Don't try to stand up. Just roll." He slid off his jacket and threw it down into the snow. Then he took off his gloves and tossed them after it. "You can put those on when you get there. You'll be needing the warmth. Now, you ready?"

She nodded. "As ready as I'm going to be."

He squeezed the tips of her fingers and whispered another prayer under his breath. Then he slid his hand underneath her torso. She felt his hands feeling their way along the curve of her back. Slowly, gently, he worked his fingers in between her body and the metal casing.

"Okay, I've got it. When I say 'go', you're going to roll down those stairs right here, down to the ground. No hesitation. No thinking. Just roll. Ready?"

"Ready."

"Go."

She rolled down the stairs, her body beating hard on the frozen wood, expecting at any moment to feel the searing heat of an explosion consuming her body.

She landed on her face in the snow, pulled herself up, and looked back at her rescuer.

Joshua was kneeling on the porch, both hands pressed against the small land mine, in a position almost like CPR. Faint morning sun fell from above, onto his head and shoulders.

He had a strong nose and a tender mouth. Even through the folds of a dark fleece she could see the broad cut of his shoulders. The faint scruff of day-old shadow brushed the lines of his jaw.

She slid on his jacket and gloves and felt the residual warmth fill her limbs.

"Now run," he said. "Get as far away from here as you can. You won't get a cell signal anywhere on this road, but if you turn left you'll reach civilization eventually. To be totally honest, I don't know if I'm going to be able to defuse this thing. If I do, I'll come find you."

She hesitated. So he'd had no actual plan other than taking her place and substituting her life with his?

An engine roared from beyond the trees. From inside the house, she could hear the dog barking again, and only then realized it had ever stopped. Someone was coming.

"Samantha!" Joshua's voice sounded clear and commanding. "Get out of here. Now!"

Headlights shone through the trees, then flashed across her face.

She ran.

The glare of approaching headlights filled Joshua's view. As much as he hoped it wasn't a foe, he hated the idea of putting any friend in the situation he'd found himself in. Samantha had disappeared into the shadows and he couldn't see where she'd gone. He looked down at the small land mine he was now keeping depressed with both hands at once. He'd seen this kind before. Round and beige, his buddies in ordnance disposal said there were thousands of them still littered over the world's abandoned battlefields. Not that he ever expected to find one in Canada. Or be in the situation he was now.

Whoever Samantha is, she knows her land mines.

A truck pulled down the driveway. The engine cut and doors slammed.

The headlights faded slowly, as a lightly bearded man started down the driveway, with the kind of smooth, confident walk Joshua had secretly spent a good chunk of his teen years trying to copy.

Thank You, God! A prayer filled his heart. Alex and Zoe were back. Alexander Fletcher had been Joshua's best friend since kindergarten. While Joshua had been overseas serving his country, Alex had tried studying first to be a doctor, then quit to become a paramedic, before dabbling with the idea of a career in law enforcement and spending a few years teaching high school math and gym. He was the smartest man Joshua had ever met, even if Alex had spent years going through life like a boat searching for its anchor. But he'd finally taken up Daniel's offer of moving to rural Ontario to help him start up Ash Private Security.

Alex was one in a million. And there wasn't a single person on earth Joshua knew more about, which just might save them now.

"Code yellow jacket," Joshua shouted. "Big, huge, code yellow jacket."

It was their own private in joke, which they'd used to warn each other of serious trouble ever since a teenaged Alex crashed Joshua's first truck when a wasp flew in the window.

Alex froze. "Zoe, stay back." His arms shot out to keep her from coming any closer, looking like an umpire calling a runner in safe. "Josh? Where are you? What's going on?"

"On the porch. Holding a live land mine."

"And you went with 'code yellow jacket'?"

"Figured you were more scared of wasps than explosives." Nothing like a friend you could joke with when you were one wrong move away from death. "It's pressure sensitive. Small blast radius. I'm leaning into the detonator right now, keeping it down. If I let go, it explodes."

"Okay." Even in the pale morning light he could tell Alex's face had gone white. "Zoe, we got a situation."

"Tell me what you need." Zoe leaped out of the vehicle. She was tiny, barely four foot eleven, with the kind of sharp, single-minded focus her stepbrother had occasionally lacked. Her chin-length hair was currently black with a few streaks of red. A world-class athlete in both gymnastics and mixed martial arts, Alex's sister had been Daniel's second private security recruit. It was her dog, Oz, who'd been barking just moments ago. Couldn't hear the pup now.

"All right," Joshua said. "Zoe, open the kitchen door, get Oz out of here, drive until you get a cell phone signal and call the police. Tell them we've got a live land mine. If you run into a beautiful blonde woman wearing my leather jacket, her name is Samantha. I think she needs help, but I don't necessarily trust her and you probably shouldn't either."

He could feel his teeth grind at the very thought of warning them against Samantha. But what did he know about her really? Nothing. Except that she'd appeared on his friend's porch tied up tight with an explosive underneath her. And after witnessing too many foolish men implode both their military careers and personal lives over meaningless war-zone infatuations, Joshua had learned there was a whole lot of truth to Gramps's warning against trusting any attraction sparked in a moment of crisis.

Zoe didn't even pause, she just ran for the side of the house. Alex started quickly but carefully toward the steps. "And what do you want me to do?" Alex asked.

"Find something we can replace my weight with. Something big and heavy. It's a pressure trigger and it's armed, so if I let go of it something else needs to take my place."

"Should I ask who this beautiful blonde is and how you got into this mess?"

"I don't know who Samantha is," Joshua said. "I just found her here on the porch, freezing cold and tied up on top of a land mine. She said she was a fact-checker. And yeah, she's staggeringly attractive—unbelievably so—like the kind of woman you don't just run into in real life. So if there's any chance I'm dreaming, now would be a really great time to pinch me."

"I'm afraid not."

"Didn't think so. Anyway, whoever Samantha is, she's lost, she's in trouble and she's absolutely terrified of whoever left her here."

Oz shot past. The dog tore down the driveway. Seconds later, Zoe and Samantha came back around the corner of the house, dragging a bag of cement between them.

"I take it that's her?" Alex's eyebrow rose.

"Yeah, but I told her to run."

"Hey, I'm Alex." He ran toward them and grabbed the middle of the bag, sharing the load. "I see you've met my sister, Zoe."

"I did." Her voice strained under the weight. "I'm Samantha. Hope you don't mind but I let the dog out. Sounded pretty frantic. Found this by the garage. Thought you could use it to counter the pressure on the land mine."

Joshua didn't know if he was more relieved, impressed or amazed by her plan. Not that he exactly liked the idea of her doing the exact opposite of what he'd just told her to do to save her own life. But she was quick-thinking. And brave. He had to give her that.

Slowly, Samantha, Zoe and Alex hauled the cement up to the bottom of the steps, then started climbing up toward him. They reached the top step and he directed them until they were holding the bag right over his hands. Then they lowered it, inch by inch, until the weight rested on top of his fingers, pressing them deeper into the trigger. He took in a sharp, painful breath.

"Now, you all go. Run. I'm going to inch my fingers out of here and we'll all pray it doesn't blow."

The three of them ran back down the steps. Alex and Zoe made it almost as far as the truck before stopping. But Samantha stopped in a faint pool of light at the bottom of the stairs.

"Samantha, please." His eyes searched her face.

"You just saved my life. I didn't hear one quiver of doubt from you when you were doing this for me. Your nerves were rock steady."

Yeah, but that's only because I was so totally focused on saving you I blocked out the danger that I was in.

"So, logically you'll be safer if I stay," she went on. "Just do what you did with me, only do it in reverse and don't blow up. I believe in you."

He inched his fingers out slowly, one by one, feeling the weight of the unmixed concrete sliding in to take their place. First one hand, then the other slid out until the bag of cement lay across the porch in front of him where Samantha's body had been just moments ago.

He let out a long breath and slid his gun back into his holster. Then he stood up and carefully inched his way around the bag. He could hear Alex clapping but didn't look at him. Instead, his eyes locked on where Samantha was still standing at the bottom of the stairs. A smile of relief crossed her lips.

"I told you to run," he said.

"I told you to run first."

"That's not exactly the same thing."

I'm a professional soldier. It's my job to save people. And you're just whatever "fact-checker" is.

He took another step. The porch creaked.

The bag of cement shifted behind him.

The land mine detonated.

THREE

An explosion shook the frozen air. Smoke and flame billowed upward, filling Samantha's view. For a moment she felt rooted in place as if time had frozen around her.

Then she saw Joshua, leaping between her and the flames. He caught her in his arms and pushed her down to the ground. They landed in the snow, his body sheltering hers. Her head tucked into his neck. Debris rained down around them. The world seemed to roar with the sound of glass shattering and wood splintering.

Then the world stopped shaking and all Samantha could hear was the steady beat of Joshua's heart and his ragged breath inches from her face.

"You okay?" he asked. His voice was gruff, but soft. He slid off her into the snow.

"Yeah, you?"

"Yeah." He stood slowly, reached for her hand and helped her to her feet.

"Everyone okay?" Alex called. He and Zoe were running toward them.

"Yes." Joshua let go of her hand. "Thankfully the land mine wasn't that strong. Though I'll have to have a word with Daniel about reinforcing his windows if he wants to convert this place into a safe house."

Both men smiled at his weak attempt at a joke, but she could see the worry filling their eyes. A hole lay on the porch in the place where her body had been. Judging by the mass of broken glass, the land mine had launched the cement bag through the front window. A high-pitched alarm was ringing from somewhere inside the house.

"I'll go sort out the alarm." Zoe ran toward the back.

"Make sure the police are called, if the alarm doesn't do that automatically," Joshua called after her, realizing as he said it she was probably already thinking two steps ahead of him.

Alex's eyes ran from Joshua to Samantha and back again. "I'm going to go see if I can find something to tape the window up with until we can get some new glass installed."

He disappeared after his sister. The alarm

stopped. Joshua and Samantha walked around the side of the house. Rays of winter sunlight stretched across the snow around them. They stepped through the back door and into a warm welcoming kitchen. Even the shattered window on the other side of the house couldn't dampen its hominess—and its heat.

The clock over the stove read eight fifteen. The smell of fresh bread and unbrewed coffee grounds filled the room. She slid off his jacket and gloves. "Thank you for these. I hope you're not frozen."

"I'm fine. There was enough adrenaline to keep me plenty warm." Joshua kicked off his boots and brushed the snow from his hair. It was light brown, the color of maple syrup, short on the sides as she'd expect of a soldier, but just long enough on top for someone to run their fingers through. The eyes that now searched her face were the same hazel-green as a forest pond. Muscles rippled through his shirt. But somehow they didn't make him look hard, only strong. An old-fashioned coffeemaker stood on the counter. He filled it with water. "I was going to make myself coffee. But would you rather have tea or something like that? There's a whole box of different colored ones around somewhere.

Also, there's fresh banana bread. I threw it in the bread maker last night."

"Coffee is perfect, thank you." A slight smile crossed her lips. "Your mother raised you well."

"Nope." His smile grew tight. "Grew up in an all-bachelor home with just my gramps and dad. But they taught me well enough."

Her tongue felt heavy in her mouth, like she should apologize. But before she could even start to figure out what to say, he kept talking.

"The closest hospital and police station are over an hour away." He leaned back against the counter and slid his hands into his pockets. "But Alex used to be a paramedic and Zoe's probably giving the police directions on how to get here as we speak. Now, you said you have no idea what happened or what you're doing here?"

"That's right," she said. "I'm a journalist from Toronto. My job is researching and fact-checking mostly. Making sure those hotshot *Torchlight* reporters can actually back up what they're writing about with cold hard facts. I was heading into work this morning to grab a tablet when I was abducted. But I don't remember what happened exactly and I don't know what whoever did this to me wanted."

Light dawned behind his eyes and with it came an almost reflexive grin that warmed something inside her.

"If you're a reporter," he asked, "does that mean you work with Olivia Ash?"

"Yes! Olivia is my editor at *Torchlight*."

"This is her country house." His eyes grew wider. "My friend is her husband."

No doubt she'd feel terrified later about what that could mean about the motives of the men who'd kidnapped her. Right now, she was just too relieved to discover she was in the home of someone she already knew and trusted.

"They're staying at their apartment in the city until the baby's a little bigger and the roads improve," he added. "Which you probably know given you work together. I'm just thankful that I was here, and the house wasn't empty."

She dropped into a chair as the sudden joy she'd been feeling evaporated just as quickly. "Yeah, me too."

"So, I'm guessing whoever did this to you wanted to get your boss's attention and didn't know Olivia wouldn't be here. Did she have you working on anything dangerous?"

"I see pretty much every story before it goes to the press," she said, "and I fact-check all the big ones. I'm like the factual safety net for our front-line reporters. It's my job to comb through each article and circle every fact with a red pen that a reader might question, just to make sure our backs are covered. Of course, our reporters write about everything. But in my job, almost everything I work on involves something criminal. I even built what they call an 'intranet' database, called ATHENA, that pulls all of our stories and background research together in one place on our online server, where only *Torchlight* reporters can see it. It even includes pointers on understanding human behavior, criminal pathology and body language to help reporters figure out whether or not the people they're interviewing are telling the truth. It's like a simplified version of the ways police detectives learn to analyze criminal traits."

But what would police make of her inability to remember how she'd even gotten there? She couldn't remember a single thing about how or where they'd grabbed her.

It had been the same back in college when that guy from her floor had broken in. She'd barely remembered anything afterwards. And while they'd eventually caught the culprit and he'd admitted to being high at the time, thanks to her faulty memory they'd only given him a slap on the wrist. She'd been forced to switch schools and start over.

Then, the nightmares had started.

Joshua pulled his right hand out of his pocket. There was something gold and glittering between his fingers. It was a ribbon. And with a start she realized it must've been the same one that her abductor had gagged her with. He looked at it carefully, holding it by the very edges.

"If you were on your way to work, it's entirely possible they were after any *Torchlight* staff they could get their hands on, and you just happened to be in the wrong place at the wrong time," he said. "But it's also entirely possible this has nothing to do with the newspaper you work for and someone tried to abduct you for a completely different reason. Does this mean anything to you?"

He laid the ribbon over the table in front of her and for the first time she saw blurred streaks of what looked like Magic Marker. Between the snow and the struggle whatever had been written on the ribbon was smudged beyond recognition, except for the last two words:

always,
Magpie.

His eyebrow rose. He didn't even have to ask the question.

"I have never heard of Magpie." She could feel her lower lip quivering but it was more from frustration than fear. She *should* know. If there was someone out there upset enough at *Torchlight*'s reporting to abduct and threaten one of their journalists, she was exactly the one person who should already have a whole file of stories and research on them in the ATHENA database. "I have no idea who or what that is."

"Neither have I," he said. "Someone twisted enough to kidnap a woman and plant a land mine under her doesn't just spring up out of nowhere. Is there anyone else you can think of who'd want to hurt you? Work situation? Family? Relationships?"

"My parents are retired and live in Montreal. They're pretty awesome people and I can't think of any reason why anyone would want to hurt them." Tension pulled along her shoulder blades. She could tell he was probably trying to help but sorting out her own mind was hard enough without having someone firing questions at her. "Work is great, really. I'm probably what some people would call workaholic, but to me that's a good thing."

"A land mine is a very specific weapon," he said, "and using the Christmas ribbon was very specific, as well. Someone was clearly trying to send a message. Any other problematic relationships?"

"No. No relationship problems." Unless someone counted the fact she got completely tongue-tied every time she tried to explain to Eric that she just wasn't hotwired to spend that much time with an enthusiastic extrovert. "Really, I'm just a happy, quiet workaholic with no enemies."

Except the dangerous and unknown Magpie. *Why don't I know who that is?*

There was a knock on the door frame. She turned. It was Alex. He glanced down at the ribbon warning lying on the table. "Sorry to interrupt. Zoe got through to the police. They've asked us all to stay put and to please try to keep from talking to each other about what happened until we've all been interviewed separately by police. I'm guessing they don't want us colluding on one version of events or getting our stories muddied. Even accidentally."

Yeah, that was pretty standard for police investigations.

"Thank you," she said, finding the words totally inadequate for the situation.

"We've figured out Samantha's connection to the Ashes," Joshua said. "Samantha works for Olivia at *Torchlight News*. We should call Daniel and Olivia too and let them know what's going on."

"Good idea." Alex sat down beside Samantha. "How are you feeling?"

"Bit shaken, but not bad. Thankfully, I wasn't out in the cold that long before Joshua found me."

"Can you hold out your hands for me?" Alex carefully checked her hands for frostbite. Then he slid a small flashlight out of his pocket and checked her eyes. "Any headache? Nausea?"

"No."

Alex ran one finger slowly back and forth a few inches in front of her eyes. She followed it with her gaze. "Stomach upset? Double vision?"

"No. I'm rattled, obviously, but physically I feel fine."

"How's your memory?" Joshua asked. "Any short-term amnesia? Memory gaps?"

Her brain froze as she turned to look at him. Why had he asked that? Those hazel-green eyes were focused intensely onto hers. A dozen thoughts cascaded through her mind that she couldn't figure out how exactly to turn into words.

Yes, I'm having memory gaps. Everything between the moment I realized I'd forgotten my gloves and almost arriving here in the van is a blur. It's frustrating. It's terrifying. The same thing happened years ago, after someone broke into my dorm room, and it was like I could only remember it in the nightmares which plagued me for months.

She broke his gaze and look down at the table. "Yes, and I know we shouldn't talk about the details of how I was abducted or anything that's happened until the police have questioned us. But I won't lie. My memory is really patchy. Like I said, I don't know how I got here."

There was a long pause and an ache in her chest, like something inside her heart had started to open just a bit, and she was waiting for it to clang shut again.

She hadn't admitted having memory gaps to anyone for a very long time. Not since she'd tried to report the attack in college to some very unsympathetic people in campus security.

But the very fact Joshua had asked gave her the faint hope that he might actually get it.

"It happens." Joshua pushed off the counter.

"Don't worry. I'm sure the police will figure out what's going on."

No. He didn't understand.

Early-afternoon sunlight glistened off the frost on the corner of the windshield as Joshua steered the car down the tree-lined parkway into downtown Toronto. A vicious snowstorm was scheduled for later, but for now the city seemed to sparkle in the sun. He glanced sideways at Samantha. Her face was turned toward the passenger-side window. His borrowed leather jacket enveloped her body. Something inside him ached to ask her what she was thinking.

They'd both talked briefly to Daniel and Olivia on the phone and then the police had arrived at the farmhouse before they'd even finished breakfast. Four vehicles and six officers, including a forensics team. They'd quickly taken over, questioning each of them privately and going through the scene, until finally they'd given Samantha permission to go home and allowed the others to replace the glass in the window and nail some boards over the hole in the porch.

It had been an odd, unsettling experience, standing on the sidelines, watching people in uniform do their thing. Between his training and his military service, he was used to being in the thick of it. He was comfortable there. Dad had always been a cop and had no plans to retire. Gramps had served in the military. Both had instilled in him a deep respect for authority and a strong sense of duty. It had been pretty clear by the time he reached high school that he was expected to follow in either one man's footsteps or the other.

He didn't imagine Gramps would've thought much of Ash Private Security or Daniel hiring Alex and Zoe as bodyguards. In fact, he pretty much knew what Gramps would've said: *So, instead of having a real job, your friends are just gonna run around and play at being cops? I suppose now you're gonna want to quit your job and join them?*

Gramps had never thought much of Alex, and Joshua couldn't even guess what he'd say about tiny, feisty Zoe protecting someone. It wasn't that Gramps didn't respect women. He just believed they needed caring for, and had cared deeply for the ones in his own life—and so he had been devastated when his wife had died in a traffic accident when Joshua's dad was small. That pain had only compounded when Joshua's dad had grown up to then marry a woman who'd abandoned her husband and child when Josh was just a toddler.

His grandfather's voice rang in his ears. *See, Joshua, losing your heart to a pretty face is always a bad idea. Beautiful women are all flash bang, but no staying power. Go meet a good, decent, steady woman, who's not too pretty, not too fancy, not in any trouble, and happy with a calm and boring life. Trust me. The human heart is dumber than dirt when it comes to falling in love.*

It had been a comfortable drive to the city despite the rambling in his brain. They'd driven more or less in silence. When they'd first gotten into his rental car, the radio had been blaring Silver Media's early-morning radio show. The host had been loud and grating, like he'd overdosed on caffeine. But Samantha'd instantly leaned over and switched it off, which he was happy for. Since then, the car had been filled with nothing but the rumble of the engine and the tires crunching on the snow-covered road.

"Toronto police recovered my bag, by the way." Samantha's voice drew his attention back into the present. "An officer told me, just before they gave me permission to leave. They found it in an alley Dumpster almost halfway between my apartment and work. I also called my landlady Yvonne while you were being questioned and told her police would be stopping by. I gave the police permission to look around my apartment in case they find something there. But considering where they found my bag, police don't think either my apartment or the office is a crime scene, and it's most likely I was grabbed off the street. Unless someone kidnapped me elsewhere and threw my bag in a random Dumpster to confuse things." She ran both hands through her hair. "I should've told you earlier, but my brain's just been so overwhelmed it's like I couldn't process the information right away."

He nodded. "That happens. Sometimes when something big happens on deployment it's like everyone's sleepwalking for hours afterwards. Might take days before people are able to start talking about it."

Of course, most never talked about the hard stuff. No matter how many times they all got reminded that therapists and chaplains were available for a reason.

"I should get my bag back sometime today," she said, "and still manage to catch a train to Montreal tonight. I was supposed to leave this morning, but the good thing about the train is I've got options. As long as I make it to the station by noon tomorrow I'll make it home for Christmas Eve dinner. How about you? When do you leave?"

"I'm due back on base December twenty-seventh," he said. "I'm going to spend Christmas morning with Alex and Zoe—probably Daniel, Olivia and the baby too—and then head up to Barrie after lunch for a really late dinner with Dad. He's a cop and tends to work Christmas, so that the officers with young kids can be home with their families. I'll take up a big plate of turkey leftovers for him, and we'll celebrate together after he gets off work."

Dad would ask him right off the bat if he'd decided whether or not to reenlist when his term was up in June. And if he said no, Dad would be expecting a pretty good answer why.

She nodded. Like he'd just answered a more important question than the one that she'd asked. "So, you don't come from a military family?"

"My grandfather served, but when he was widowed, he transferred home to Canada to raise my father. I have such a huge amount of respect for him, for both him and my dad, in fact. Gramps used to say God put us on this planet to protect those who couldn't protect themselves. He's the reason I enlisted."

Lake Ontario glittered ahead through a maze of skyscrapers.

"You can get off here." Samantha pointed to the right.

He took the exit, and drove through the quirky mishmash of shops, expensive condos and older buildings that made up downtown Toronto, following her directions until they reached a thin, standalone town house between two warehouses. The lights were off. A sign in the window read *Torchlight News*. He pulled into a narrow alley and parked between the garbage cans and a fire escape. His eyes scanned the silent building. "It looks closed."

"It is closed." She unbuckled her seat belt. "But like I told you, my laptop died so I'm going to pop in and borrow a tablet so I can keep working over the holidays."

"Are you sure that's wise?"

"You mean because some unknown threat that calls itself Magpie tried to kill me today?" She swiveled on the seat. "I might have data on this Magpie thing lurking in my database somewhere that could help the police catch them. Magpie has probably done this before and will do this again, if nobody stops them.

I can match my experience against other crimes and maybe find a pattern. Like you just said, we have a responsibility to protect others."

She hopped out of the car and closed the door behind her.

Yes, but in this scenario, you're the person who needs protecting. He followed her around to the front of the building. She punched a code on the front door and it swung open. The entrance space was tiny. A door marked Publishing lay to his right. A second labeled Editorial lay dead ahead. She opened it to reveal a narrow flight of stairs.

"I hear what you're saying," he said. "But you're not the authorities. You're not the police. It's not your job to find or stop criminals. You're the victim."

Samantha paused, her hand on the door leading up to the editorial offices.

"Do you have any idea what the solve rate for violent crimes is in this city?" she asked. "Sure, it's better than a lot of places, but it's definitely not one hundred percent. Do you know how often *Torchlight* journalists have given the police key information they need to make those arrests? Or the role that journalists even play in investigating crimes the police don't have the resources or remit to investigate? My job is facts. I find them, sort them, connect them, make sense of them and see patterns. I'm good at that. So, yeah, I'm going to spend my Christmas researching crimes like the one I just survived. Even if you think I'm too useless, or helpless, or whatever it is you seem to think I am, to do my job."

It was the longest string of words he'd heard her say since they'd met, and it had all bubbled out of her with a passion that knocked him back a step. He opened his mouth but couldn't think of what words to say to that, so closed it again.

"What if the police never figure out who Magpie is?" she went on. "It's not like I've given them much of anything to go on, except 'Strangers grabbed me somewhere, for no apparent reason. One smelled like he smoked a lot and the other had missing teeth.' I told you back at the house, I don't remember being abducted. I don't remember anything useful. I remember leaving my apartment. I know I ended up tied up in a van at Olivia's house. The last thing Olivia needs, with a new baby! Everything else is missing. Like my brain's ability to remember anything more than that has been broken." A fire flashed like gold in the dark of her eyes. "But that doesn't mean I have to just sit around now and wait for someone else to save me. You don't get to decide I'm nothing but a helpless victim. Nobody does. Not even Magpie."

Then before he could even think of anything else to say to all that, she turned on her heels and started up the stairs. He watched her legs disappear up the stairs but didn't follow. She'd told him back at the house that she couldn't remember being abducted, and he'd presumed it was just the normal haze people had when their adrenaline was pumping. Most people don't pay attention to detail at the best of times and so tend to forget a lot.

But Samantha isn't most people.

He sat down on the steps, stretched his legs out and dropped his head into his hands.

Dissociative amnesia. Short-term memory loss. Those were two phrases he'd heard far too many times over the years to describe the way the brain protected itself from remembering things that happened in times of intense trauma. Over the years he'd heard person after person he'd served with, and officer friends of his father's too, describe the symptoms. They talked about "memory gaps" and "brain fog," and the sense that certain memories had been stolen from their minds. It hadn't even registered that's what she'd meant when she'd told him that her memory was patchy. He couldn't even begin to imagine how frustrated and scared she'd felt, or how insensitive he must've sounded. He let out a long breath and prayed, "God, please just help me figure out how to best help her."

Then he pulled his phone out of his pocket and dialed Daniel.

"Hey, Josh!" Daniel whispered. "Olivia and the baby are asleep. How is everything going? Alex told me you were taking Samantha home?"

"We decided to stop at the newspaper on the way." Joshua stood up. "Apparently she wants to pick up some kind of computer tablet thing so she can do some research on whoever this Magpie is."

Daniel chuckled. "Yeah, Olivia predicted she would. I know we didn't talk to Samantha long, but Olivia knows her well. Apparently, Samantha's tenacious when it comes to collecting and understanding information."

Joshua started up the stairs to the second floor. "I wish the police had offered her some decent ongoing protection instead of just letting her leave there with nothing but a phone number to call and a recommendation for counseling from Victim Services."

"I'm sure the police do too," Daniel said.

"But they can't assign an officer to every single person in trouble." Which is where Ash Private Security came in.

"Do you have a phone number or contact details for Theresa Vaughan?" Joshua reached the landing to the second floor and found a hallway of closed doors. "Alex's former fiancée? The therapist? Last I heard she was volunteering with Victim Services."

"I'm pretty sure that Olivia does. Why? Do you think Samantha should talk to her?"

"Maybe."

A crash sounded above him. A scream filled the air.

Samantha!

"Daniel!" he said. "I think we have an intruder at *Torchlight*. Call nine-one-one!"

He stuffed the phone in his pocket and pelted down the hallway. A second scream came from above now. This one was louder, angrier, like a wildcat fighting for its life. The door at the very end of the hall was open. He dashed through and found himself pelting up a second, narrower flight of stairs that opened into a huge, open-concept space with steeply slanted ceilings and a scattering of cluttered desks.

The image of a bird spanned the sloping wall ahead of him in dripping spray-painted strokes of black. Beneath it a graffiti artist's signature tag read: *Hermes.*

Two more lines of scrawl curled in uneven strokes along the adjacent wall.

The Magpie says,
You've been warned.
Delete—

The words cut off in a trailing line of paint. Joshua could feel the hackles rising on the back of his neck.

Delete what?

A muffled cry came from his right. He turned. Samantha stood still in the entrance of a long narrow alcove. Instinctively his hand reached out to her, a question forming on his lips. But as he stepped toward her, the shadows shifted, and he saw why she stood frozen. A man grasped her tightly around the neck from behind. A white hoodie and a buglike painter's respirator mask covered his face. Hermes's arm tightened around Samantha's neck, yanking her back in a choke hold.

FOUR

Instinctively Joshua's hands rose in front of him, hoping the universal sign of non-aggression would buy him enough time to figure out what was going on, and how to get Samantha out safely. Quickly he surveyed the room, his battle-ready gaze rapidly taking in the details. Winter light and cold air streamed through the alcove, which Joshua guessed must lead to the fire escape. The scrawl on the wall was still wet and dripping. A single overturned chair and a few papers strewn on the floor signaled a small-scale struggle. But the room hadn't been ransacked. The mask that hid the intruder's face was the kind of plastic respirator mask worn by graffiti street artists and people doing home repairs. Despite the heavy leather boots on the young man's feet, the baggy hoodie covering his head implied he was a common thug, not a military operative.

"Hermes" kept one arm around Samantha's

neck. The other hand was buried in his sweat-shirt pocket. Whatever that hand was holding inside the pocket, he was pushing it hard against Samantha's side. So, Hermes had a weapon. A knife? A gun? Another explosive? Whatever it was, there was no way the man would miss hurting Samantha with it at that range, and there was no way to safely disarm him in a space that narrow.

So, Hermes. I'm guessing you didn't expect to find anybody here and don't have a plan.

"Hey, it's okay." Joshua kept his voice steady. "It's all going to be okay and nobody needs to get hurt. Can I call you Hermes? That's your graffiti tag, right?"

No answer. Gray eyes glanced up suspiciously over the top of the respirator mask.

Joshua risked taking a step toward him, his voice level and his hands still slightly raised. "You don't want anybody to get hurt, do you, Hermes? You're not a bad guy. You're not looking for trouble. You just came here as a messenger from Magpie to paint something on the wall, right?"

With every step he could feel the empty space on his hip where his service handgun would normally be. But Canadian gun laws being what they were, even he didn't have a permit to carry a service weapon while on home leave.

He glanced at Samantha. His eyes took in every inch of her form. Her clothes were disheveled. She hadn't given up without a fight. But her limbs now shook. Her gaze darted around the room.

Look at me, Samantha. Please, I know your brain is going to want to switch off and let the fear take over. But fight it. Stay focused. Stay with me.

Hermes took another step backward, dragging Samantha after him by the throat.

Come on, Samantha! Please! I need your help to get us both out of here alive.

Hermes slunk deeper into the alcove, blocking out the light. Samantha's eyes closed in what he hoped was prayer. Joshua's silent pleading turned to prayer too. *God, please help me defuse this situation! I'm going to have no choice but to rush Hermes. But if I do, I'm putting Samantha's life in danger.*

Hermes spun Samantha around sideways and for a moment seemed to get caught as he jostled for room in the narrow space. Then, with a cry, Samantha tumbled backward out the balcony door. Joshua sprinted across the room. The graffiti artist yanked a gun from his pocket and fired. Instinctively, Joshua dropped to the floor and rolled, as the sudden bang and flash seemed to fill the room. But the sound of the bullet's impact never came. He crouched onto his toes and looked up. Hermes closed his eyes and fired again. No recoil. Joshua almost snorted. Hermes was shooting blanks. Joshua vaulted over the second desk and charged. Hermes turned on his heels and ran out the door after Samantha. But before Joshua could even reach the alcove, he heard a crash and an angry scream of pain filled the air.

Joshua ducked into the alcove, ran through and came out on a small balcony leading to a fire escape. He blinked. Hermes now lay flat on his back. Shards of pottery were strewn around him on the icy wood. Dirt covered Hermes's body like soot. Joshua turned and saw the reason why. Samantha stood by the fallen graffiti artist. Pale sunlight fell over her face. Fierce defiance flashed in her eyes. The remains of a heavy clay vase were still clutched in her hands. A jolt rippled through Joshua's heart like it was attached to jumper cables.

Samantha had grabbed the vase and broken it over Hermes's head.

Sirens sounded in the distance. Samantha's

eyes snapped to Joshua's face. "Please tell me you called nine-one-one."

"Daniel did."

"I've got the gun from him." She held it up. "But he was just firing blanks."

Huh. So she knew something about both guns and land mines.

Hermes was groaning. The young man pulled himself onto his hands and knees. Joshua pushed him down and pinned him with an arm against his throat.

"Who are you? What are you doing here? Who sent you? Who is Magpie?"

He yanked off the respirator mask. Frightened eyes stared up into his face. Something inside Joshua's heart lurched. Hermes was clearly overwhelmed and terrified. Had Magpie even told him the gun was loaded with blanks? Joshua sat back on his heels, loosening the pressure on the boy's throat. Someone that unseasoned and scared probably wasn't going anywhere.

He turned to Samantha. "Do you have any idea who this is? Have you seen this guy before?"

"Sorry, no."

"Is it possible he was one of the men who abducted you this morning?"

"I don't think so. Similar age, I think. I

barely saw the one guy's face but it was very scarred and he practically reeked of tobacco. The other one definitely talked like he had teeth missing."

"All right, I'll watch him until the police come," he said.

"I'm sorry."

"Don't worry about it," he said. But there was something in her voice and about the way she'd said "sorry" that made him look back at her face. It was like she was being hard on herself for not knowing more. Something inside Joshua's chest suddenly ached to just give her a hug and tell her that everything was going to be okay. "Look, I'm sorry if I sounded insensitive earlier. But—"

Out of the corner of his eye, Joshua saw Hermes's hand dart toward something on the ground. He spun back. But it was too late. Hermes slashed at him with a small, jagged pottery shard that just barely missed his jugular. Instinctively Joshua reared back, releasing his weight on Hermes's body, as he lunged to grab the shard. Hermes kicked up, hard, one boot just managing to catch Joshua in the chin. Pain exploded in Joshua's head, not enough to make him let go, but enough to let Hermes slither back on the icy wood and twist from his grasp.

"Stay back!" Joshua yelled to Samantha. He leaped to his feet. "And stay out of the way."

But it was too late. Hermes leaped onto the fire escape and bolted down the stairs.

She watched as Joshua leaped over the ledge onto the fire escape below, skipping the first flight of stairs entirely. He pelted after Hermes. Their footsteps clanged on the metal steps. Samantha grabbed the edge of the balcony with both hands. Everything inside her wanted to chase after them. But Joshua's words still seemed to echo around her in the frosty air. *Stay back. Stay out of the way.* And why would he even want her to try and help? She'd fought as hard as she could against Hermes, but he'd still overpowered her. She'd broken a vase over Hermes's head and then he'd managed to grab a shard of it and use it as a weapon. Joshua already made it perfectly clear he doubted she could be any use at all in stopping Magpie.

He'd never understand. Joshua had height, brute strength and military training. She had two left feet and a tongue that tended to either babble or freeze. He'd probably thought her big speech on the staircase had been pretty ridiculous. But, whether he got it or not, she really had joined *Torchlight* to make a difference.

Hermes was still running down the fire escape. The graffiti artist might not know his way around guns, but he was wiry and fast. This probably wasn't the first time he'd vandalized something and run from getting caught. Hermes's feet hit the ground. He pelted across the pavement. Joshua was only a few steps behind him. In a second, he'd caught Hermes by the shoulder and swung him around. The youth thrashed. But Joshua yanked his arm back, pinning it behind his back and holding him firmly in place.

"I don't want to hurt you." Joshua's voice echoed in the concrete alley. "I promise you that. I'm just going to hold you until the police get here. But if you keep fighting me, I'll be forced to tighten my grip."

The rest of his words were swallowed up in the sound of police sirens. She stood there for a long moment, looking down at Joshua as he calmly but firmly held the squirming vandal in place. Then she turned back toward the office. Any moment now, cops would be all over the place and *Torchlight News* would be a crime scene. If she was ever going to take a look at what had happened with a critical, journalist's eye, it had to be now.

Carefully, she took a methodical look at Hermes's unloaded gun. It was a Glock. The serial number had been filed off and it looked like someone had tried to tamper with the barrel in order to make it something more dangerous than it already was. But they'd done it so badly she doubted the gun would ever be much use to someone who was actually trying to hit their target. *Illegal handgun. Modified by an amateur. Loaded with blanks.* It was the kind of weapon a stupid kid might use to try to intimidate someone, but never actually intend to fire. Thanks in part to Canada's strict gun laws, Toronto police had warned recently of an increase in replica and damaged weapons being used to commit thefts. Sometimes just waving a weapon around was enough to get someone to give a thug what they wanted. Trust criminals to get creative.

But it was even more evidence Hermes had been sent as a messenger not a killer. She could almost feel her brain storing the information like memory chips sliding into mental slots.

She walked back through the alcove into the office. The smell of wet paint still lingered in the air. Hermes had graffitied two walls, one with a warning message and the other with a huge, crude bird. Quickly she took a picture of both with her tablet and uploaded them to the ATHENA database on the *Torchlight News* server. Then she slipped back onto the balcony just long enough to zero in on Hermes's face as Joshua held him pinned waiting for the police. She saved that picture too. As long as she had computer access and her *Torchlight* password she could access ATHENA no matter where she was in the world. Then she grabbed an electronic stylus pen and started for the stairs.

Questions burned in her mind. She paused on the second-story landing, opened a fresh document on the tablet and jotted them down with the stylus, using them like an electronic pen and paper, just as if she was sitting in the corner of an editorial meeting listening to a reporter talk about their big new exposé. Why would Magpie send a graffiti artist to break into *Torchlight News* and scrawl a warning on the wall the same day they kidnapped a journalist? Why do both? Vandalism was vile, yes, but if a reporter was pitching this story in an editorial meeting, methodical Samantha would have pointed out that threats usually escalated in severity. That is: normally the warning came first, then the attempted murder.

She wrote "Does Magpie have a vendetta against Torchlight?" in block letters at the top of the page and underlined it twice. No doubt Olivia would get every single journalist at the newspaper to report in on what they were working on. Maybe the mysterious Magpie would emerge from there and the paper would know what it did to land on Magpie's radar.

She crossed the second-floor landing and froze. Olivia's office door was ajar. She could hear the creak of someone's weight shifting on the old office floorboards and computer keys clacking. There was somebody else in the building. Her heart raced through her chest, so suddenly she found herself battling to breathe. Were the police in there already? But if so, wouldn't they have announced their presence? The door swung open quickly. She was face-to-face with a stranger. He was short, in plain clothes and probably forty, with a square face and a red baseball cap.

And familiar. So very familiar. And she didn't know why.

"Who are you?" she demanded. "What are you doing here?"

The man hesitated. Then suddenly he lunged for her tablet computer and tried to yank it from her hand.

"Drop it!" he shouted.

Was he kidding?

"No! Get out of here! The police are on their way!" Her grip tightened on the tablet. For a moment, she thought he was going to succeed in pulling it from her hands. But then, while all his body strength was focused on the tablet, she kicked him as hard as she could. He swore and let go. She yanked the tablet back, hearing the edge of the case crack as she wrenched it from his hands. She ran down the stairs to the ground floor, panicked tears building in her throat.

"Joshua! Help!" She grabbed the front door handle, Joshua's name escaping her lips even before she could finish yanking it all the way open. "There's another intruder in the building!"

"Ma'am! Get away from the building!" Strong hands grabbed her shoulders and pulled her away from the door. Samantha looked up into the face of a senior officer whose hair was tied back in a tight bun at the nape of her neck. Half a dozen more officers rushed past them into the building. "Are you all right, ma'am?"

"I'm… I'm fine. Thank you, Officer. But there's a man in the building. Second floor. He's short and wearing a red baseball cap. I don't know if he's armed." Samantha looked around. Police vehicles and people in uniform seemed to be spilling down the streets in both directions.

But she couldn't see Joshua anywhere.

FIVE

Half an hour later she was sitting alone in the small, quirky café across the street from the *Torchlight News* offices, watching the foam swirl in the top of her coffee and trying not to wonder where Joshua was. Was he being questioned by police? Had something happened with Hermes? He wouldn't have just taken off without saying goodbye. She was certain of that. Well, almost certain. After all, it wasn't like he'd signed up to do anything more than give her a ride back to Toronto. Even that he'd only done because she'd suddenly landed on the doorstep in danger. She sighed. Truth was, there was so much data she simply didn't have on the man. Despite the odd effect he seemed to have on her heart.

Sprigs of holly and pine bows curved along the window frame. Her coffee smelled like nutmeg and cinnamon. She held the side of the mug tight with one hand, feeling the comforting heat of the ceramic seep into her palm. With the other, she idly ran an electronic stylus along the computer tablet. She'd let the officer who'd questioned about the break in look it over. But with all of ATHENA's data saved on *Torchlight*'s online server, there wasn't much saved on the actual tablet to look at, and she knew her job well enough to know she didn't have to relinquish it without a warrant. Fortunately, the officer seemed satisfied to let her keep it.

Slowly she sketched out everything she could remember about the second-floor intruder, using the pieces of her memory like puzzle pieces. The lines of his square, clean-shaven jaw. Deep-set eyes. The shape of a holster on his hip. She focused on every tiny detail she could remember. The two kidnappers and Hermes may not have sparked anything in her mind, but there was something about this snoop that was familiar and she was going to figure out what.

Where have I seen your picture before, stranger? What did you want with my tablet?

Are you Magpie?

Bells jingled and clattered as the café door opened, bringing a gust of cold air in with it. She looked up, embarrassed at just how much part of her hoped to see Joshua standing there.

"Olivia!" Samantha jumped up as a woman with flame-red hair and a voluminous white scarf crossed over to her table. Even dressed in a tracksuit without any trace of makeup on her skin, the *Torchlight* editor seemed to beam with both happiness and confidence. Samantha gave Olivia a gentle hug, and was surprised at how strong her embrace was in response. "What are you doing here? I thought you'd be home with the baby!"

"She's with Daniel." Olivia unwound her scarf and dropped into the seat farthest from the window. "Police needed someone from *Torchlight* to come in and confirm the state of things. Our apartment is only a few blocks from here and to be honest we really needed a walk." A tired but genuine smile crossed her lips. "We finally decided on a baby name by the way—Abigail Rose."

"It's beautiful." Samantha sat down opposite her. Olivia leaned her arms on the table and squeezed her hands.

"How are you doing?" Olivia asked. "Are you holding up okay?"

There was an understanding in her voice that tugged at something deeper inside Samantha, reminding her that there were times others in the *Torchlight* family, including Olivia herself, had faced criminals, danger and threat of death to get the story. I'm okay." Samantha squeezed her back and let go. "Not great. Still kind of shaky. But I'm okay. Thank you for asking and understanding."

"Do you remember Theresa Vaughan?" Olivia asked. "We did an article on her a few months back. She's a therapist and counselor, who does a lot of work with Victim Services."

Samantha nodded. "I think so." The woman Joshua had mentioned. Why did her thoughts keep turning to him?

"I gave her a call about what happened to you today. She and I have talked in the past about running something for the staff. She's willing to meet with you before you leave town. She's really good at helping people sort out their memories and feelings about trauma."

Samantha sat back and wrapped her arms around her chest. But what if she didn't have any concrete memories? Could Theresa still help her then?

"Her office is just on the northern edges of Toronto, about half the distance between here and the farmhouse," Olivia went on. "Today's supposed to be her last day in the office before the holidays, but she said she's free to meet you at four, or first thing tomorrow. It's not on a public transit route. But Joshua knows her. I'm sure he'd be happy to take you."

Did that mean she'd already discussed it with Joshua, wherever he was?

"Thank you. I'll think about it. Have you asked the rest of the staff about Magpie?"

"I talked with senior staff, and we sent out a joint email to the *Torchlight* crew, informing them of what had happened to you, asking them to let us know everything they'd been working on recently, and if they had any idea on what Magpie is. We also asked them to take extra precautions with their own safety until this is sorted." Olivia looked down. "Police didn't try to confiscate your tablet?"

"They asked to look at it and I let them," Samantha said. "Enough to let them feel satisfied there wasn't any harm in letting me hold on to it. But I reminded them that they couldn't take it from me without a warrant."

Olivia nodded. A smile crossed her lips. "Good job."

"Thanks." She smiled back. Samantha tapped the screen, waking it up from battery saving mode. Her sketch of the snoop's face appeared from the darkness. She turned it around to face Olivia. "Recognize him? I caught him rummaging around in your office and he tried to steal my tablet."

"Police told me there'd been someone in my office. Nothing seemed to be stolen. It looked like he'd tried to hack into my computer, but didn't get past the password." Olivia looked down at the sketch. "No, I've never seen him before."

"Well, I have," Samantha said, "or at least I saw a picture of him. When I close my eyes I can see his face on a piece of paper. But I don't know what piece of paper that would be. Is it possible he works for a rival media organization?"

Olivia's eyebrows rose. "Why?"

"Because that would explain where I'd seen him before. There has to be some reason why Magpie is trying to intimidate *Torchlight*. The media world is very competitive. It's possible there's a *Torchlight* investigation they're trying to force us to stop. Or maybe they're trying to scare us out of business altogether."

Joshua stood on the sidewalk on the opposite side of the street and waited for a break in traffic. He could see Samantha through the window. Her blond head was bowed toward the table. She was talking to someone whose face he couldn't see, but he could tell that she was animated about something. A curious smile illuminated her face, like she was both confused by a problem and eager to solve it. He sighed.

How could he feel so lukewarm, and even apathetic, about the major life decision he had to make about his military future? Yet so interested in finding out more about this woman he'd just met? There was this quality about her that he couldn't even begin to put into words. She was like something a guy would only see high above him on a billboard. Not just sitting there in a coffee shop, with his old battered leather jacket draped around her shoulders. Despite all the dire warnings he'd had growing up about not letting his foolish heart distract him from the things that really mattered, nothing in his life had ever really prepared him for what it was like to feel something like this.

A baby stroller brushed alongside him and instinctively he turned to offer to help it down off to the curb, before looking up to see the tall, dark-haired man with serious eyes behind it.

"Daniel! Hey, I wasn't expecting to see you until Christmas." Did that mean Olivia was in the coffee shop with Samantha right now? He looked down through the clear plastic weather cover to the tiny bundle inside, but could barely see the baby under the mound of blankets.

"The police needed a senior person from the newspaper to come reset the alarm." Daniel gave him a quick one-armed hug while keeping his other hand firm on the stroller. "Olivia was the closest key holder. Plus our apartment's only a ten-minute walk from here and I really needed a walk. We all did. Although, to be honest, I was hoping to wait until Abigail was a little older before taking her to her first crime scene."

Joshua fought the urge to chuckle. The Daniel Ash he'd known had such an overprotective streak he never would've been okay with his wife and infant coming within a mile of a crime scene—even if it was just a break and enter. When Joshua had heard of his whirlwind romance with the red-haired spitfire of an editor, he'd wondered how Daniel's protective nature was going to handle being married to someone so independent and strong in her own right. Now, looking in the new father's eyes, he was suddenly reminded of the first time he'd run his bare hand along the huge stone walls of one of the ancient fortresses in the Holy Land, and been shocked to discover something so strong could have such soft edges.

"Olivia's still keeping in touch with what's happened at the paper while she's on maternity leave," Daniel added. He reached one hand inside the stroller and adjusted the blankets. "She wanted to talk to Samantha in person. Olivia took your suggestion and called Theresa. The good news is Theresa's agreed to meet with Samantha. Either today at four or tomorrow at ten, whichever she prefers."

Joshua's eye turned back to the café. Samantha's elbows rested on the table. Her gaze was still focused on something in front of her.

"I have something to ask you," Daniel said. Joshua looked back. Daniel's eyes were watching his face. "Olivia feels a huge responsibility for Samantha. The newspaper's like a second family, and I think we're all agreed that Samantha shouldn't be alone until this is settled, or at least until she boards her train to Montreal. She thinks, we think, somebody should be protecting her."

"You mean a bodyguard?" It was the logical conclusion for both Daniel and Olivia to jump to. Still, something about it irked him and he wasn't sure what. "I agree, someone should watch her. But like you said, police don't have the resources and manpower to escort around every woman whose life has been threatened. You've just had a baby. I don't think you should be away from Olivia and Abigail. For all we know their lives are also in danger. While personally I would trust both Alex and Zoe with my life, and I'm sure they'd both agree to do it, I don't think either of them have really spoken to Theresa since she practically left Alex at the altar. Foisting that on them suddenly two days before Christmas might be asking a lot. But at the same time the idea of just hiring some stranger through the phone book terrifies me."

"I know," Daniel said, "which is why I was hoping you'd do it."

"You want me to be Samantha's bodyguard?" Joshua ran his hand over his jaw. He would've almost laughed, if the situation wasn't so serious.

"Just for today," Daniel said. "Only if you want to and if she's okay with it. Just be a friend who has her back. She may not want to go talk to Theresa."

"She *should* go talk to Theresa, though," Joshua said.

"I know," Daniel said. "Olivia may be her boss, but she can't force her to get counseling or accept private security. I get the impression from Olivia that Samantha really values both her solitude and autonomy."

So, the man who didn't think he wanted to be a bodyguard was going to protect the woman who didn't think she wanted protecting.

"Yeah, I'll do it," Joshua said. What else could he say? "It just makes sense. I know where Theresa works and I definitely know how to watch for hostiles and manage threats. Plus, I know how the cops work and think, so I won't be tripping all over their investigation if they want to ask her more questions. I hope when you get Ash Private Security off the ground you get someone to give Alex and Zoe some guidance on how to deal with the authorities too, so the client fully benefits from both. You know, doubly protected."

A mild smile crossed Daniel's lips that said something more than Joshua was able to read. The lights changed and traffic paused. They crossed the street. Joshua matched pace beside the stroller, his right hand resting on the handle at the front until they reached the other side. Then he carefully helped Daniel lift it back up onto the sidewalk in front of the café.

"Thank you," Daniel said. "Obviously, Olivia, Abigail and I are going to be staying at our apartment in the city until this is settled. Trust me, the idea someone would deliver a threat targeted at my wife, on my own doorstep is not something I take lightly. She's encouraging all her staff to take precautions. I asked Alex and Zoe if they'd be more comfortable moving out of the country house, but they pointed out there's no reason to believe whoever threatened Samantha will return there, and that it would be easier to protect than a busy city location."

"I agree," Joshua said. The country house had good sight lines and a safe room in the basement. It was hardly the kind of place that was easy to sneak up on now that they suspected someone might be coming. "Although breaking into the newspaper office is a pretty big sign that whoever's behind this has *Torchlight* itself in their sights, not Samantha personally. It's just a bad coincidence she happened to be here, twice." And he was the one foolish enough to let her head up to the top floor of the newspaper office alone.

The door swung open, and that's when Joshua realized Samantha and Olivia were already on their way out to meet them. He stepped back, vaguely aware of Olivia greeting him before brushing past him to be with her husband and baby, and then of Daniel saying something to Samantha. But somehow, it was like the only detail he could truly focus on was the way Samantha's eyes flitted to his face and then down to rest somewhere just right of his shoulder, as if there was something hidden there she didn't want him to read.

"So, you survived." Samantha smiled. "I was wondering where you were." She held her computer tablet to her chest and he realized with a start that she was still probably even more determined to continue researching Magpie now.

"I did," he said. "The police had a lot of questions for me. I heard from Daniel that you're going to be meeting with Theresa later."

"Maybe." Her gaze dropped farther down his arm until it was resting on his hands. "For now, I'm heading to the police station. Hopefully they'll release my bag and keys so I can get into my apartment."

Goodbyes with Daniel and Olivia were quick. They were eager to get back home. Thick snowflakes had begun to swirl down sideways from dark clouds moving in on the horizon and the baby had begun to stir. A few minutes later, Samantha and Joshua were sitting back in his car again. She held the tablet so tightly her hands almost quivered. He could tell there was something on the tablet she wanted to show him, but whatever it was it also looked like she wanted to wait until the car was moving. He eased the car out through an alley still crowded with cops and gawkers, then started driving.

"There was a second intruder in the building," she said after they'd cleared a few blocks. "He was short with a square jaw. Again, nothing about him reminded me of the two men who'd abducted me. He was in Olivia's office. He looked kind of like this." She turned the tablet toward him. The light turned yellow ahead and there was a black sports car tight on his bumper who probably wanted him to push through. But he eased to a stop anyway and then looked down at the sketch.

"You drew that?"

She nodded. "Yeah, did you see him? Do you know if he was arrested?"

"No." He didn't much like the idea that she could've been hurt by somebody else while he was busy sitting on Hermes. "But I was pretty much focused on our graffiti artist and then being questioned by police."

"I'm pretty sure I've seen him before," she said. "Or at least a picture of him. But I don't know where. I wondered if he was from some rival media company. But that's just a guess."

The lights changed. He started driving again. The black sports car stayed so tight on his bumper, he'd probably hit them if Joshua braked quickly. He hated downtown driving.

"Did he hurt you?" Joshua asked.

"No, I'm fine." She shook her head. "He didn't even touch me. He just tried to steal my tablet, but I kicked him hard and he ran. He wasn't much of a fighter. I hope police got him."

"Why would he want to steal your tablet?"

"I don't know. Like I told you, my laptop was refusing to work for me, so I just picked this up to access the *Torchlight* online server. Looked like he tried to hack into Olivia's computer but couldn't figure out her password."

"Is it possible that somebody intentionally damaged your laptop?"

"You mean like someone intentionally tricked me into downloading a virus? Or that somebody hacked my laptop and damaged it?"

"Either." He could see the police station up ahead on the right now. The black sports car was still tight on their tail. He took a sharp left and dodged quickly but smoothly between two approaching vehicles. Then he headed down a block, cut right and accelerated through a yellow light before it turned red. The black sports car kept pace. Samantha's hand brushed his arm as her eyes rose to the rearview mirror.

Yup, they were definitely being followed.

SIX

Joshua scanned the mirror. The man's face was hidden under a baseball cap. Something inside the soldier's chest burned to lead the trailing vehicle somewhere away from innocent bystanders, then pull over, confront the man and find out exactly what he wanted. But there was no way he'd put Samantha in that kind of danger. No, the smartest thing to do was pull directly into the police parking lot and find out if the man following them was foolish enough to challenge them there.

"Obviously we've got a guy on our tail," he said, "and he's really persistent. I'm going to pull in at the station." Joshua circled the block, put his turn signal with plenty of forewarning and then pulled in to the police station. The black car hesitated, then drove past. Joshua got a glimpse of a short man, a square jaw and a red hat. "Recognize him?"

"Yup." Samantha let out a long breath then

sat back against the seat. "Same guy who was rummaging around Olivia's office and tried to steal my tablet. Well, there goes the hope that he was arrested. But at least now I've got a license plate and car model to report. Are you going to wait it out here and see if he comes back around? I'm probably only going to be in the station for a minute."

"No." Not that he was a fan of the idea of letting the man get away either. He switched off the rental car. "I'll come in with you."

Did she know that Daniel had asked him to be her unofficial bodyguard? If not, how should tell her? He waited just inside the front entrance of the police station while she collected her belongings—and lodged a report about the man in the black car. So much for a quick ride home.

When they finally exited, he noticed that Samantha's bag was bright blue, leather and looked like something that might've been sold in the sixties. Maybe it had been. She held it on her lap and looked through it as they drove to her apartment. He followed her directions into a narrow maze of back alleys that ran behind buildings. Between the parked cars, garbage cans and Dumpsters the lines of sight were terrible. If these were the alleys that Samantha had walked through to get to work long before the sun was even up, he could see a dozen ways someone could have grabbed her and forced her into a van without being seen. She directed him to a small but crowded grid of spots behind a gabled, four-story building that looked like it had once been a sorority house. Then they sat in the car with the motor running and heat pouring out of the vents.

"It's all here," she said, finally. "My wallet, my credit cards, my cell phone and the keys to my apartment. Everything. Down to the last bill and coin. They definitely weren't trying to rob me. Unless they stole my coat. I was kind of hoping police would tell me it had turned up in the garbage too."

"What kind of coat was it?"

"It was beautiful, lined, vintage green wool. I'd picked it up secondhand in Kensington Market." She unbuckled her seat belt. "I tend to shop secondhand whenever I can. But why steal my coat and leave my wallet?"

"There might've been some kind of evidence on it they wanted to destroy," Joshua suggested. "Something you'd picked up or gotten on you, like oil, dirt or blood?"

"It's possible, but there was no blood on the rest of my clothes or body. And I was walking through the exact same alleys I walk through every day, so there shouldn't be any kind of unusual transfer. Unless I'd physically been somewhere out of the ordinary before ending up in the back of the van."

"Or maybe you'd just taken the coat off before they kidnapped you."

"On the street? Why would I randomly take my coat off, in December, while walking to work?" Her voice trailed off as sudden tears rushed to her eyes. She brushed them away before they could fall.

He turned toward her. "Hey, it's okay to be scared."

"I'm more than scared." Her eyes flashed. "I'm confused. I'm frustrated. I'm angry. I'm overwhelmed with questions that I can't begin to find answers to. Starting with why did somebody kidnap me and dump me on Olivia's doorstep? I'm not the one who goes chasing stories all over town with a microphone and a camera. I'm the one who's quite happy sitting quietly in the corner of the room, listening to all the loud, gung ho reporters compete over whose stories are going to make it above the fold this week, fully confident that whatever gets picked I'm going to make sure it's all meticulously accurate. It's my job to check facts, to verify data, to know things. Here, I don't know anything." She pressed the heels of her palms against eyes. "I don't even know how I got from an alley into a van."

"Come here. It's okay. It's going to be okay, I promise." He slid his arm over the back of the seat. Her head tumbled against his shoulder. He hugged her tightly, feeling the warmth of her body inside his arms and the brush of her hair against the stubble on his cheek. "You're incredibly brave and incredibly strong. You're going to get through this."

She raised her head. But she didn't pull away. Her face was so close to his he could almost count the flecks of gold in her eyes. Her breath was soft and fast against his skin. He realized just how much he wanted to know what it would be like to kiss her and how very easy it would be to lower his mouth onto hers.

"You'll get through this and don't have to go through this alone." He could hear his own voice growing hoarse as he spoke, as if everything she was feeling had started to build in his own throat. Her eyes closed. "Look, I never thought I'd be anybody's bodyguard. I don't know why. I just had it drilled in me to always serve in a unit and never try to go off alone. But, like I told Daniel, I'm going to do everything I can to have your back."

Her eyes opened wide. She slid back.

"Bodyguard?" There was an added question in her words that he couldn't quite read. But he could feel it, sitting there between them like a trap ready to spring. "You mean, you're here with me now because my boss's husband asked you to follow me around?"

Why was she making this sound like a bad thing?

"Well, yes," he said. "They asked me to make sure you got to Theresa's okay and that you had somebody watching your back."

"Of course they did," she said slowly. "That's very kind of them, and of you. I haven't actually decided if I'm going to go see Theresa or just head home to my folks."

"Well, you should really think about going to see her," he said. "Short-term amnesia is really common for people who've been through major traumas. Like soldiers and the victims of violent crime. Counseling can help a lot. And Theresa's really rather wonderful at helping people with your condition."

"My condition." She frowned. "Of course. It was your idea that I make an appointment with Theresa, because I told you my memory was giving me trouble and you were asked to look out for me."

She said it calmly, simply. Not like she thought he'd done anything wrong. More like she was just now realizing the answer to a

puzzle and that she wished she'd figured it out
before. She got out of the car. He followed.
Shades of white and gray now blocked out
the previously sunny sky. Thin, skeletal trees
grew in a strip of dirt by the back door. Garbage floated in a swamp of water and slush
that filled the Dumpster to his right. Dark
gray painted over the brick walls, covering
what he guessed had probably been graffiti.
The narrow building was four stories tall with
what looked like two or three apartments on
every floor. Despite the weather, a window
on the top floor was cracked open.

"Do you see that?" He pointed up to the
window. "Whose apartment is that?"

"It's mine." A flush rose to her cheeks.
"When I left this morning, I hardly expected
to be out all day. My former neighbor had a
cat who still pops by every now and then to
cry at my window for food. I think it climbs
up a tree and leaps over to my window ledge.
Her ex-boyfriend, Eric, found out, felt guilty
about it, and so drops by food for it every now
and then. So, sometimes I prop my window
open a few inches and leave a dish of food
on the counter. I'm on the top floor and those
trees won't support a person's weight. You'd
have to be an actual cat to break in."

His eyes lingered on the window for a moment. Despite her optimism, there were probably plenty of ways someone could break into her apartment and before he left he'd do his best to find and address each one.

The keys jangled in her hand. She unlocked the building's back door, and they stepped into a narrow hallway that led to a large, spotless front entrance lobby. A huge bulletin board by the front door was plastered in layers of photocopied signs, warning against the dangers of everything from not recycling to letting in unidentified guests. He followed her up the stairs past at least a dozen more posters. "Your landlady definitely runs a tight ship."

"Definitely." Her footsteps creaked as they climbed. "Yvonne used to be a dorm mother at some kind of boarding school for troubled kids, years and years ago. Not sure if it's the kind that kids went to voluntarily or more like a detention rehabilitation place. I guess the tendency to try and overpolice her tenants comes from that."

By the time they hit the second floor the posters had sort of blended together in an unending stream of words and color. He could imagine tenants stopped even reading them after a while.

"Yvonne's a bit kooky," she went on. "Very

glamorous actually, in her own way. But I'm pretty sure she's lonely. She'll make excuses to drop by my apartment to check on one thing or another. Then she'd end up lecturing me on finding a good man, unlike her good-for-nothing ex-husband, or telling me some long-winded sob story about how her darling son doesn't appreciate all she does for him."

"You're paying rent to live here," he said. "Even if she owns the building, there've got to be limits to the kind of rules she can set."

"Oh, there are." Samantha smiled. "I've researched them well and I know Yvonne sometimes pushes it a little. But it's also a decent, safe, clean apartment that I can actually afford, walking distance from my work. Do you know how impossible it is to find one of those in this city? I'm not about to risk losing it."

To be fair, a landlady who had a habit of trying to micromanage her building wasn't necessarily a bad thing considering everything Samantha had been through. If whoever had kidnapped her had been loitering outside the building, Yvonne might've seen it. He'd have to make a point of meeting her. Although, it probably wouldn't hurt to close Samantha's window first.

They reached the top floor. Unlike the others, this one had only two doors, one on each side of the landing. A beautifully delicate wreath of dried leaves, twigs and velvet ribbon lay on the door to their right. A small sparkling gift bag hung on the door handle. Before he could reach for it, she glanced at the card then reached inside and pulled out a small, giftwrapped box.

"Everything okay?" His eyebrows rose. "Is that something maybe I should take a look at?"

"It's just a Christmas present from Eric. We were supposed to meet for coffee this morning and he must have come by looking for me." She slid the bag, note and gift-wrapped box into her skirt pocket without unwrapping it. Crimson brushed the top of her cheeks. "Trust me. It's nothing to worry about."

Right. Whatever was in the box it sure didn't look like cat food. She'd told him when they'd met this morning that she had no problematic relationships. Now, he was discovering that she sometimes left her window open for visits from a part-time cat, her landlady was odd and she was supposed to have coffee this morning with someone who brought her gifts. But she was already fumbling with her keys and he got the impression that she wouldn't take it well if he asked to see whatever was in the box.

There was only one other door on the landing. It had an eviction notice taped to it.

"So that would be where the cat lady lived?"

"Her name was Bella." Samantha was still fiddling with her keys as if she'd momentarily forgotten how to slide them into the doorknob. "And she wasn't a cat lady. She was in her midtwenties and very beautiful. I think she was a model."

He was happy to see that Samantha had both a doorknob that locked and a dead bolt. Bella's door had an empty hole above the door handle where the dead bolt used to be. Her doorknob looked like someone had picked it. "How long has she been gone?"

"About two months, I think. She talked to me a bit in passing about wanting to move out, even asked me for advice on movers. But she never gave notice or even turned in her keys. She just left. One day I just saw movers in the hallway and she was gone. Apparently she sent Eric a breakup letter in the mail. He was devastated. They'd seemed really devoted to each other." She shrugged. "Yvonne eventually stuck the eviction notice up, and then finally got someone to break in. Yvonne's totally redoing the apartment in the hopes of upping the rent on it. That apartment is a lot larger than mine."

Considering the location, an apartment like this would probably go for a premium. Still, he didn't like knowing the only other apartment on Samantha's floor was lying empty. It was too...convenient.

"Welcome to my place." She pushed her apartment door open. The living room was an open square, with a kitchenette along one side. A futon couch and overstuffed chair draped in handmade quilts shared the space with a coffee table built from half a canoe. A small Christmas tree sat in a metal bucket on a table in the corner of the room. Samantha shrugged his leather jacket off her shoulders and carefully hung it on a wrought-iron hook by the door. Then she went to the small window over the sink and closed it. Besides a small empty cat-food bowl, the counter was spotless.

He reached to close the door behind him and stopped. Was it his imagination or was there a noise coming from the empty apartment across the hall? Creaking. Shuffling. Like something was trying to creep across old wooden floorboards. Was the cat skulking around its old apartment? Or was there a more human-sized pest? Whatever it was, it didn't sound like renovations.

"Hang on. I think I hear somebody in that

apartment." He left her apartment, crossed the landing in two steps and rapped on the neighboring door. "Hello? Anyone in there?"

No answer.

"I'm pretty sure it's empty." Samantha stood in the doorway to hers.

"You're probably right." He reached for the door handle. "I'm just going to check. Last thing you want is for someone to climb up the fire escape and break in through the empty apartment."

"But it's all right if you break into it?"

There was a sharpness in Samantha's tone that made him stop.

"I'm not breaking into it. If the door's locked I'm hardly going to break it down. But I will check to see if it's already been compromised. I promised to watch your back. Now I'm discovering there's an abandoned apartment on the same floor as yours?" The handle turned easily. Somebody had either broken the lock by picking it or they'd left it unlocked. "Yeah, it's probably nothing. But I'm going to have a quick peek inside. Don't worry."

He pushed the door open. The smell of dust and old potpourri filled his senses. He took a step over the threshold—just as a baseball bat swung straight at his head.

* * *

For a moment everything was happening so quickly Samantha didn't even know how to understand what she was seeing.

"Get back!" Joshua shouted. He leaped back, pulling in his stomach just as a baseball bat sliced the air inches from his body. She got a fleeting glimpse of thin hands in black leather gloves. The baseball bat smashed into the door frame. Splinters flew. "Go into your apartment, lock the door and call the police!"

Samantha ran for her phone.

"Get out of my building!" The voice was female, high-pitched and furious.

Yvonne? Samantha turned back. A glimpse of silver hair and flowing black fabric moved through the empty doorway.

"Yvonne!" She ran across the landing. "Stop! It's me, Samantha—"

The bat swung again. But this time Joshua was ready. He leaped to the side, grabbed the bat with both hands, and yanked before Yvonne had time to even let go. Her landlady's pencil-thin form tumbled through the doorway. Josh reached out and caught her with one arm before she could hit the floor.

Yvonne gasped. Long, silver-blond hair tumbled around her back. A black, red-lined winter cape wrapped around her shoulders.

The rose-tinted glasses perched on her nose made her irises look almost purple. Samantha had never known how to guess Yvonne's age, but she was definitely old enough to be somebody's grandmother.

"Yvonne, I'm so, so sorry!" Samantha cried. "Joshua! This is my landlady."

"Forgive me, ma'am, I mistook you for an intruder." He carefully set Yvonne to her feet. His right hand hovered behind her back until he was certain she was steady. But still his left hand held the baseball bat. "I can't apologize enough. This mix-up is entirely my fault."

Yvonne straightened her clothes. A scowl turned on bright red lips. "Samantha, who is this man?"

"Sorry," Samantha said again, not even certain what she was apologizing for but yet feeling like she couldn't apologize enough. "This is Joshua. He's my..." She hesitated as words flitted past her tongue. *He's my bodyguard, my rescuer, my hero...*

"Her friend," Joshua supplied. "My name is Corporal Joshua Rhodes. I'm serving with the Canadian army, but home for the holidays. In fact, Samantha was just showing me her apartment and telling me how much she likes living here."

His tone of voice somehow managed to be conciliatory without leaving any doubt that he was the one in charge of the situation. He was still holding the bat away from Yvonne, but in such a casual way that if someone hadn't been paying attention they might've thought he'd forgotten about it.

There was something about the way he just stood there, filling Samantha's tiny landing with this sense of calm and authority that suddenly made her so very aware of his military training. That made her think that maybe, just maybe, here was a man who was even capable of helping her slowly pry back whatever it was that had locked up her heart so tightly she could barely feel it beating. If only he was staying in her life beyond today. If only he saw her as more than just a problem to be fixed and a favor to be sorted.

"We should all go to my apartment, sit down and talk," Samantha said. "We've all been through a lot. I'll make some tea." It was bad enough the horror with the Magpie almost cost her life and job. She wouldn't let it threaten her apartment too. "Please, Yvonne."

Her landlady sniffed and for a moment Samantha thought she was going to argue. But instead she just turned the lock on the back of the damaged doorknob and closed the door. "Come on, then. We might as well talk this out."

Samantha breathed a sigh of relief. Yvonne tended to run hot and cold. Samantha would make tea and find some cookies. Joshua would probably be charming and listen to Yvonne's stories. It was hard to imagine anyone disliking him for long. She led the way into her small, one-bedroom apartment. "Have a seat. I'll put the kettle on."

"What kind of trouble are you in exactly?" Yvonne stayed standing. "I don't appreciate being woken up in the early hours by a phone call from one of my tenants warning me to expect a visit by police." She cut her eyes at Joshua. He was sitting on the very edge of the armchair and still hadn't let go of the bat. "Or being attacked by some stranger in my own building."

Okay, so apparently Yvonne wasn't going to bounce back that fast.

Samantha took a deep breath, and tried to weigh how to tell the landlady the truth, without being too dramatic or telling her more than she needed to know. Figuring out the right words to say was never Samantha's strength even under the best of circumstances.

"I was…" Samantha started. Then paused.

Kidnapped? Attacked? Waylaid? Abducted? Tied up with Christmas ribbon and left at her boss's house with an explosive device under the small of her back? "The details are really fuzzy, but I was accosted by someone on my way to work this morning. They forced me into a vehicle, drove me around and dumped me at my boss's house."

Yvonne took in a breath so sharply it was like someone had sucker punched her. Her face blanched.

"Now, I wasn't badly hurt, by any means. I wasn't really hurt at all," Samantha added quickly. "Fortunately, Joshua was there to help me and he's agreed to hang around and make sure I'm okay until I catch a train home to see my family."

"And the police?" Yvonne's voice rose. "What do they say? You know they came stomping around here, asking me to let them in to rifle through your apartment."

Yes, she'd given the police permission to search her apartment that morning and had told Yvonne to expect them.

Samantha glanced around. Well, if police had been "stomping" through, certainly nothing looked touched. It was more likely they'd just looked around long enough to confirm it wasn't a secondary crime scene and left.

"Well, thank you for letting them in," she said. "I'm sure all they were trying to do was eliminate this as a possible crime scene." And certainly she didn't see anything out of place. "But we're pretty sure what's going on is totally related to my work and nothing personal. Someone's unhappy with my newspaper, for whatever reason, and I happened to be a staff person they could threaten. A couple of intruders broke into my office too. I'm sure it's absolutely nothing you need to worry about."

"Your job. Of course." Yvonne snorted. It was a disdain-filled sound that seemed to emanate from the back of her throat. Then she turned to Joshua as if suddenly deciding he was a potential ally. "This girl works too much. Too hard and too much for that tiny little newspaper. I come up the stairs at night and all I hear is *tap, tap, tap, tap, tap.* You know, a few days ago I saw a nice young man come in here, in a good suit, carrying a big shopping bag. He tells me he's here to bring her cat food and cook her lunch. Then a few minutes later I see him walk back down the stairs. He tells me she's too busy for lunch. Too busy for lunch on a Saturday, with a handsome young man who has a good job." She rolled her eyes. Her finger jabbed the air toward Samantha. "This one likes her job so much she turns down a man like that? It's like she has no heart beating in her chest. None. She will end up old, bitter and alone."

Samantha winced. She should be used to Yvonne's ranting by now. After all, she was probably doing nothing more than projecting her own pains and disappointments onto Samantha. Yet something about her sharp words stung deeper than she liked to admit. Was her heart faulty? Was she even capable of making a connection with someone like Joshua?

"Do you often come up here to the top floor at night?" Joshua asked.

Yvonne's mouth parted slightly. Then it snapped shut like she'd just been caught out.

"No. Maybe. I don't know. I get noise complaints about the tapping."

"You received a noise complaint about Samantha's typing from Bella across the hall, before she moved out?" Joshua wasn't letting it rest.

Yvonne crossed her arms in front of her chest and didn't even bother answering. Something cold and stubborn flickered behind her rose-colored lenses.

"You mentioned a young man coming by to invite Samantha for lunch," he pressed.

"That would be my friend Eric," Samantha said. "The one who used to date Bella.

He dropped off some cat food last Saturday and offered to make me lunch. I told him I was busy."

But Joshua barely glanced at her. Instead he leaned forward, as if he found Yvonne's complaints fascinating.

"Do you often question your tenants' visitors about who they are and what they're doing in the building?" he asked. Again, his voice was so calm it was almost unnerving. Was he trying to get information out of Yvonne? Did he think he was being helpful?

"Shouldn't I protect myself from strange men roaming around in my building?"

"Have you had a problem with intruders before?"

Yvonne crossed her arms. "Maybe."

"Or maybe you didn't," he said. "Maybe you just like bullying your tenants and take it for granted they'd rather move out than challenge you or take you to landlord tenant tribunal for wrongful eviction?"

Just like that the darks of Yvonne's eyes snapped from ice to fire. "You're wrong. You don't know anything. Maybe I am tired of some creepy man wandering around outside at night, taking pictures, trying doors, spying on me!"

"What creepy man?" Joshua stood up and

Samantha could practically hear the hackles rising at the back of his neck. "Are you saying you called the police about someone *spying* on this building?"

"The police? Bah! What would the police do? I warned my tenants! I saw someone spying on my tenants, I caught a man trying to break into the building, so I put up flyers, telling them not to let any unidentified people into the building!"

Samantha could feel her jaw drop. "You did *what*?"

But Yvonne had already turned on her heels and stomped out of the apartment. Her footsteps echoed down the stairs.

"Do you have any idea what she's talking about?" Joshua asked.

"No." Samantha shook her head. "I mean, maybe I saw something about watching for strangers. But she does that all the time. It's hard to explain Yvonne. She latches onto things. She's a bit paranoid. She puts up flyers for everything."

Joshua sighed and shook his head. "I'm sorry, I wasn't actually trying to upset her. I was hoping that if I pushed her a bit something would click and we'd get somewhere helpful. You never want to discount a potential ally. But, you really need to move out of here and find a new apartment."

Before, that tone of confidence and authority in his voice had been reassuring. Now it rubbed her exactly the wrong way.

"I like my apartment. Despite Yvonne's ranting it's probably safer than a lot of buildings. I can afford the rent. I can live here on my own. It's walking distance from my work, which is nearly impossible to find in the city—"

"Here!" Yvonne strode back into the room, waving a torn blue notice in her hand that looked like it had been stuck to the wall under several subsequent pieces of paper. "I told you I'd warned the people who lived in my building that somebody was sneaking around!"

She slapped the flyer down on the coffee table. Samantha looked down at the photocopied face of the snoop who'd broken into *Torchlight* and tried to steal her tablet.

SEVEN

The picture was grainy, like someone had taken it hastily from a distance and then enlarged it with a photocopier. The man's eyes were hidden under the low brim of a baseball cap. His face was partially turned away from the camera. And yet, somehow Joshua still knew what Samantha was thinking before he even felt her fingers brush his sleeve. He raised his hand slightly in her direction, just enough that he hoped she'd understand he was asking her to hold the thought.

"Is this the only photo you took of this man?" he asked.

Yvonne scowled. "The only one where you can see his face. He's sneaky."

"Do you mind if we keep this?"

"Take it." She crossed her arms. "I don't care. Take it and get out. I don't want men like you in my building." She slammed the door so hard behind her that the whole room seemed to rattle.

"I suspect I know what you're going to say," Joshua said.

"Besides the fact I'm aware my landlady doesn't actually have the right to dictate who her tenants' friends are?" Samantha asked. She sighed and dropped down onto the couch. "Yeah, that's the intruder in the hat I saw snooping around Olivia's office, who tried to grab my tablet and then tailed us when we left. That's where I saw him before. It all just clicked." She dropped her head into her hands. "So, this is what it's like to suddenly remember something you'd forgotten. It feels like it should've always been obvious. But to be honest, with the number of flyers she puts up you just kind of stop noticing them after a while."

He sat down beside her. His hand touched her shoulder with the same kind of comforting tap he might give a fellow soldier heading out to battle. But then, instead of pulling away, he found himself running his hand across her back to rest in that gentle dip where her neck met her shoulders. "How are you doing?"

"Badly?" She tilted her head and looked at him sideways. Her jaw brushed against his forearm. "How do I ever begin to make sense of the fact that this man, whoever he is, didn't just break into my work but was also sneaking around my *home*? Does that mean what happened to me today wasn't just some crime of opportunity? It was actually planned?"

"I don't know." This man could've been watching Samantha for weeks before she was grabbed, and the only person who'd noticed him snooping around didn't even tell the police. Now that was a terrifying thought. This is why armies weren't loosely organized bunches of well-meaning people. "Once you've grabbed your stuff, we'll take this to the police."

"Yvonne will kill me if I send the police to question her," she said. "She hates cops. It's amazing she even let them into my space. She told me once she used to read all the files of the young people she worked with and told me this one story about how she was like a hero to these kids because the police came to arrest one, and she kicked up a fuss and refused to let them in. Maybe it stems back to whatever damage her ex-husband did to her. It sounds like he was pretty brutal. But for whatever reason, she bristles around anyone in uniform."

"A lot of people feel that way," he said.

"I mean, a huge number of people really respect the uniform too. But there've certainly been missions where it would've been easier to deal with certain people if I'd been wearing jeans and my leather jacket."

The jacket was still hung on a hook by her door. And somehow it saddened him, just a very little bit, to think that she wouldn't be wearing it when they left.

She stood up, reached into her bag, and pulled out the tablet. "I'm going to open a specific story file in the ATHENA on everything we know about what's happened—just like I would for any other big investigation. I've got pictures of the graffiti, a picture of Hermes I shot from the balcony and this picture of whoever this guy was. Plus I'll type up everything I can remember. Maybe it will connect to other crimes elsewhere. We can only hope."

She took a picture of the flyer. Then she folded it carefully and slid it into her skirt pocket. It was the same pocket that held the wrapped box that had been waiting for her when she got home. Was it from the same guy who'd invited her to lunch? And how come she didn't want to talk about it?

He could feel the questions building in his mind like a pressure headache.

"Also, I think I will call Theresa and tell her I will come see her today, if she's got time. Her place is called Palm Branches?"

"Palm Branches Counseling," he confirmed. "It's about thirty minutes north of here up the 404. Daniel said either today at four or tomorrow morning at ten."

"Today works." She glanced at the wooden clock hanging on the wall. "It might help to talk everything out with someone who's not involved in any of this. At the very least getting my own mind straight could help me with researching." She started for the bedroom. "I'm going to finish packing and get changed. I won't be long. Just make yourself at home. There's coffee in the cupboard and some milk in the fridge. If anything happens…go ahead and take care of it."

The bedroom door closed behind her. The lock clicked. He leaned back onto the couch and prayed. *God, please help me protect her.*

He opened his eyes again and found himself looking at her small Christmas tree and realized with a start that it was still alive. He sat up and took a better look. The tree was about three feet tall and potted in the earth of a festive clay pot. He couldn't remember the last time he'd seen an indoor Christmas tree that was still growing. He ran his fingers along the branches, feeling the needles prick the pads of his fingers and the supple springiness of branches that were still full of life. Every decoration from the popcorn strings, to the knitted sheep, to the ugly painted bird peeking out from deep in the branches, seemed handmade. He'd gone through more than one Christmas overseas and so gotten used to plastic trees and fake snow. But that didn't mean he'd liked them. Artificial things had always rubbed him the wrong way. Artificial people had too.

The realness of the tree suited Samantha. Her home was full of antique things, secondhand things and things that she'd made or that someone had made for her. Things he'd imagined that she'd selected carefully and wouldn't let go of easily. No wonder she'd seemed so sad about her one-of-a-kind coat.

Her cell phone started to ring, rattling its way across the canoe table.

He leaped up. "Your phone is ringing."

The phone slipped off the table and clattered onto the floor. The ringing stopped. He bent down and picked it up.

"Samantha? Hey? You there?" A voice filled the room. It was male, young and charming. Either the call had connected when the phone had hit the floor or he'd accidentally answered it when he picked it up. "Hello? Hello?"

"Hey," Joshua said. The call display showed a local Toronto number but no name. Yet something about the voice sounded oddly familiar. He held the phone to his ear. "I'm very sorry. This isn't Samantha. I'll go see if she's free—"

"Who is this?" The charm was gone. Now the voice was suspicious.

"My name's Joshua. I'm a friend of Samantha's."

And who are you?

"What are you doing answering her phone?"

Joshua gritted his teeth. Okay, he could be polite to this man, whoever he was, no matter how much he disliked his tone.

"Sorry, Samantha's in the other room and I accidentally answered her phone. Hang on, I'll try to get her." Joshua knocked on her bedroom door twice. "Samantha? Hey, I'm so sorry, but your phone fell off the table and I accidentally answered it."

No answer. Just the sound of running water coming from what he guessed was an en suite.

"So she's there?" the voice said. "Then let me talk to her."

"She's occupied. Can I take a message?"

"How do I know that you didn't just steal her phone?"

"Look, buddy." Every fiber of Joshua's nerves bristled like a dog who'd just sensed a skunk skirting up the drive. "I'm in her apartment. She just went into the other room and—"

"You're in her apartment? What are you doing in her apartment?"

Now, he could feel his fingers itching for his weapon. "Can I take a message and get her to call you back? I'm sorry, I didn't catch your name."

"How about—"

"How about you just tell me who you are and I'll make sure she knows to call you back?"

He could practically hear the other man gritting his teeth. "Eric Gibson."

That name meant nothing to him. But for some reason he thought it should.

"I'm Eric Gibson," he repeated, "the radio host, from the Silver Media morning show."

Oh. "Okay."

"I'm the man who's watching Samantha's back. I'm looking out for her. And one day I'm going to marry her."

Samantha leaned against her bedroom wall and listened to the sound of water tumbling into her en suite sink and the muffled voice of Joshua arguing with someone on the phone from the other side of her bedroom door. Had he answered her phone? No, that didn't seem like him. More likely he'd placed his own call and whoever he was talking to was arguing. Maybe Alex or Daniel. Joshua probably resented their request to take care of her.

Probably didn't help that she almost melted into his arms whenever he touched her.

What was wrong with her? For years, her body had stiffened up and shrunk away when anyone had tried to touch her like that. Now, here was a man whose touch felt like safety and home. But Joshua was in her life for just one day. Hours. Nothing more. Then they'd be saying goodbye.

Joshua was still talking loudly to someone on the other side of the door. She walked back into the en suite, added some soap and lavender drops to the steaming hot water, and washed her face and neck with a facecloth. Only then did she turn off the tap. Silence had fallen in the other room. Either Joshua had ended the call or taken it out into the hallway. She got changed into a comfortable pair of jeans and an oversize red cable-knit sweater. Then sat down on the edge of the bed and looked at the note from Eric.

Dear Samantha,

I'm so sorry we weren't able to exchange presents in person. I was really looking forward to seeing your face when you opened this. It seemed so perfect for you. Please accept this as a token of my sincere admiration and my gratitude for your friendship during this trying time. I hope we'll be in each other's lives for a long time to come.

Eric

Then she opened the present slowly. It was a bracelet. White gold by the look of it, with an inlay of diamonds and rubies. It looked old. It looked valuable. It looked like exactly the kind of thing she'd admire in an antiques store window knowing she'd never have the money to afford it. She closed the box and dropped it into her vintage, hard-backed suitcase. What was he thinking, giving her something like this? Was he this generous with all his friends? Or did he think there was something more than friendship growing between them?

Either way, she was going to have to give the gift back.

"Samantha?" Joshua rapped gently on her door. "You about ready to go? I checked the news on my phone, and they said we're in for one big huge dumping of snow today. I don't want to get caught in it and we should leave extra time to get where we're going. Traffic will probably be a nightmare." He cleared his throat. "Also your...friend... Eric... Gibson... called. He hung up without leaving a message. I get the impression he's going to call you right back."

She ran her hands through her hair, tugging it so hard she could feel it pull. Of course Eric had called. She'd probably missed a dozen calls from him already today. He'd made his grand gesture in dropping off this gift and now expected a response. She'd have to figure out how to tell him that she couldn't keep it.

"Yeah, okay, I'm on my way." She shut her suitcase, closed the clasps in place, grabbed it by the handle and then opened the door.

Joshua stood there, so close she nearly tumbled out into his arms. He held out her phone, without quite looking her in the eye, and she realized it was vibrating in his hand.

"Eric's calling you back. I presume you'll want to take it, so I'll give you some privacy. He was really irritated when I answered your phone, and suspicious. Accused me of stealing it." Joshua dropped the phone in her hand. He'd put it on Mute. "But just do me a favor and ask him where he was this morning? See if he has an alibi?"

"He doesn't need an alibi. He was on air. We heard his voice broadcasting live when we got into your car this morning. I'm pretty sure Silver Media isn't in the business of manufacturing fake radio programs to cover for their host's crimes. Besides, I'd know if Eric was one of the two men who abducted me."

Not to mention Eric had no reason to drive her out to the country and try to kill her. He cared about her. He wanted to take care of her. He didn't want her dead.

"I'll be right out in the hall if you need me." Joshua walked out and closed the door firmly.

She put the phone to her ear. "Hey, Eric."

"Samantha!" His face filled her mind. He had a wide, charming smile that brought a dimple to his chin, a mop of curly hair and remarkably bright blue eyes that Silver Media stuck on posters every opportunity they got. "Who was that guy answering your phone? Is everything alright? I was worried. I wouldn't ever want to criticize a friend of yours, but man, he had a major attitude."

Did he? Maybe. She'd have definitely said that Joshua was firm, focused and determined. She liked that about him.

"I'm sorry," she said, mostly because she

couldn't think of anything else to say. She pressed her lips together, hoping he wouldn't ask about the bracelet. She wanted to talk to him about it in person. Warning him in advance that she was about to return it would only make it harder to get him to accept that she was giving it back.

"I gave him a bit of a hard time," Eric said. "I… I probably said some things I shouldn't have. But it was in the heat of the moment and I wanted him to know that someone had your back."

"I'm sure it's fine." She glanced at the closed door. Joshua would no doubt grill her on whatever foolish thing Eric had said later. But considering everything else going on, the bravado of her former neighbor's ex was the least of their worries.

For all his persistence, Eric was as close to nonthreatening as a man could be—at least according to ATHENA. She'd never exactly set out to make Eric an unofficial test subject for ATHENA's criminal analysis and background research capabilities. But their budding friendship had been so fresh in her mind when she'd built the algorithms, and Eric had been so eager to talk about himself, that she'd found herself instinctively running him through the system. While he might be a bit too eager to please, ATHENA had determined was all but impossible he had either psychopathic or sociopathic tendencies. It would take extreme circumstances to make him resort to violence. His background check had been spotless.

"I'm so sorry I missed our coffee plans this morning," she said.

"Your landlady told me you were in some kind of trouble. She said the police came looking for you."

"I was…" She paused, prayed for wisdom and then went with almost the same thing she'd told Yvonne. "I was accosted by someone on my way into work this morning. It was sorted out and I wasn't hurt. We're fairly positive it's connected to my work. But police are looking into it. You didn't happen to see a man with a square jaw and baseball hat lurking around my apartment, did you?"

"What kind of question is that?" His voice rose. Deep concern radiated through his words. "No, of course I didn't see someone lurking around your apartment. If I had, I would've called the police. You know that! I'm worried about you, Samantha. What are you caught up in? Who was that man answering your phone?"

"His name is Joshua and he's a friend of

my editor, Olivia. Her husband, Daniel, is in private security. Joshua offered to keep an eye on me and make sure I made it on my train home today."

Eric sighed. "You know I would've done that for you. I'd have driven you around in my car. I'd have taken you anywhere you wanted to go and made sure you weren't alone."

She knew he would've. But that would've only made the imbalance in their relationship even worse. Guilt stabbed her heart. Eric was trying so hard to be her friend. "Thank you, but I'm okay. As you know I'm a fact-checker for *Torchlight News*. It looks like someone's after the paper for whatever reason. But the police are on it now."

"I don't understand why you're even working for that tiny little ragtag thing. You can do so much better. And now it's putting your life in danger. I know you love your work, but why don't you let me put in a good word for you at Silver Media? I can find you a better job, somewhere in my building. There's round-the-clock security. We could have lunch together. Plus, you'd make better money."

She paused. The Silver Media building was spectacular, with huge towering green glass windows that rose stories above the sidewalk. Walking past, every day she couldn't help but admire how it gleamed, or notice the sprawling main floor with modern art, a huge coffee shop and a bevvy of beautifully dressed people. Not to mention prominent uniformed security guards that Joshua would probably be thrilled about. She'd secretly dreamed of working there ever since she'd moved to the city. But did she really want to be beholden to Eric for a job?

"Thank you. I'll think about it." She crossed over to the Christmas tree. Someone had been touching it. She'd been very particular in how she'd spaced the decorations out. The whole tree had been balanced. Now it was lopsided. One string of lights fell crooked, sideways off the branches. Candy canes no longer hung evenly. She cast a glance at her apartment's front door, where she guessed Joshua now stood. Had he taken this bodyguard thing so seriously he'd actually been investigating her Christmas tree?

"Promise me you'll think about it," Eric said. "There are a lot of amazing internal postings in all sorts of departments. It doesn't have to be radio. The company has television, news, magazines, newspapers."

She lifted a snowman off its side and nestled it deeper into the branches. It wouldn't hurt to make more money if she was going to have to go apartment hunting.

"I'll think about it." She pushed the sagging branch up. It flopped back down again. "But they need me at *Torchlight*. I'm their only fact-checker. They count on me to be the person who knows things."

Then she saw the problem. There was some weird bird wedged near the bottom, big enough to pull the whole branch down. She peered through the branches at it. It was gold and badly painted. Like some oddly shaped turkey.

She hoped it wasn't a gift from Yvonne. Not that she could think of anybody else presumptuous enough to just walk into her apartment and stick an ugly ornament on her tree.

"Look, I don't know what time your train is," Eric said, "but why don't I come pick you up, give you a ride to Union Station, and we can talk it over while you wait?"

She stuck the phone in the crook of her ear. "That's a very kind offer, but I've already got a ride." She reached along the branches. The ornament was wedged with its heavy metal loop attached to the branch above.

"Okay," he said, "but if you need anything—anything at all—I'm here for you. One hundred percent."

"I appreciate that." In fact it was a nice change from how Joshua sometimes seemed like he was only watching her back because he had to, not because he wanted to.

She tugged the ornament gently. The bird's head snapped off. *What was this?* She gripped the heavy ornament itself by the center and yanked. With a horrible metallic clank the metal orb pulled off its hook.

No wait, it wasn't a hook. It was a pin.

She stared down at it in horror as she suddenly saw what she held in her hand.

It was a brightly decorated hand grenade.

EIGHT

"Joshua!" Every muscle in Joshua's body leaped to attention. Just seconds ago he'd been standing with his strong arms crossed across his chest and his back to the door, feeling every bit the bodyguard he'd reluctantly agreed to be. He'd been able to hear the soft murmur of Samantha's muffled voice through the closed door, but not been able to make out the words. He'd been asking himself what exactly it was about Eric that irritated him quite so much. But everything except for hot, driving instinct fled from his mind the moment he heard her voice scream his name.

"Help!" Panic filled her voice.

"I'm coming!" He grabbed the door handle and yanked so hard he could hear the wood straining. It wouldn't turn. He'd somehow locked himself out. Desperately, he eyed the door debating whether to break it down. "It's locked. Can you get to the door and open it?"

"No... I don't know..." Her voice broke. "I don't know if I can move."

That was all he needed to hear.

"Stand back!" He slammed his shoulder into the door. Pain shot through his body. The jamb split. The door flew open. He fell through after it, just managing to stay upright as the momentum almost sent him falling at her feet.

Samantha stood by the Christmas tree. Her phone had fallen to the floor.

"I found this on my Christmas tree." She stretched both arms toward him, her hands cupped around a glittering gold orb. "I'm pretty sure it's a live hand grenade."

He nodded. Step by careful step he made his way across the room toward her, until he could see the shiny object in her hands.

Tiny lettering was stenciled on it in clean, crisp, lettering.

Destroy Athena now. Or this will be your last Christmas. Magpie.

"Athena?" Where had he heard that name before?

Samantha's face had gone white. "ATHENA is my news database."

A chill spread like cold water down his back. All this was about a newspaper database? "Who knows about it?"

"Everyone who reads the paper. They did a whole profile on it when it was created. Basically it would mean wiping our servers clean and deleting every piece of information we have. The newspaper would go out of business."

"Got it." He swallowed hard, as his eyes scanned the round, heavy shape.

An M67 hand grenade by the looks of it. Common in modern war zones. Heavy. Lethal. Deadly.

"Where's the pin?" he asked.

"Attached to the tree. It was disguised as some weird bird ornament and when I grabbed it, I accidentally pulled the pin out."

"So, you're right, it could be live," he said. "I take it you're holding the handle down?"

The good thing about hand grenades—if there was any such thing as a good thing about a deadly weapon—was that once someone pulled the pin it still wouldn't go off as long as the handle or "spoon" was held down. Even then a person still had a few moments to throw it before it went off.

"Yeah, it was kind of disguised as a wing," she said. "But I've definitely got a good grip on the spoon. It was my first instinct. When I built the office database, I included a military section with a bit on hand grenades."

Of course she had.

"Where's the spoon now?"

She was holding the grenade so tightly with both hands he couldn't actually see it.

"It's sort of pressed against my right palm."

"Can I see?"

She nodded. Gently she let him move her fingers, just enough that he could see the entire shape. When he'd spotted it on the tree before the combination of the paint, clay head and surrounding branches had kept him from seeing what he was really looking at. But now, glitter and gold did nothing to disguise the shape. Yeah, there was no doubt in his mind now what this was and the kind of danger she was in.

"I'm sorry," she said. "I was so startled when the pin tore free, I dropped the phone and it went dead before I could even yell at Eric to call the police. I shouldn't have just grabbed it. I didn't even stop to think—"

"Hey, it's okay," he said. "None of this is even remotely your fault."

But it was clear that despite their hopes that Magpie's vendetta had been against *Torchlight* itself, the threat against Samantha was now personal. Very personal. He could feel her pulse racing through her skin. Her breath filled the space between them.

"There has to be a reason why someone would want *Torchlight* to destroy the ATHENA database," she said. "There has to be some information I've logged in that someone wants to get rid of. And forcing us to erase everything is less suspicious than telling us what. But who uses land mines and hand grenades to threaten and kill someone? Guns and knives are common weapons used by criminals. So are poison or rope or even makeshift weapons like household tools. But..."

Her voice trailed off. It was shaking. Her eyes locked on the hand grenade. She was scared. She was holding a live explosive. And here she was mentally stuck trying to overthink, analyze and rationalize her way out of it.

"Hey, it's okay," he said. "You don't need to understand it. It doesn't need to make sense."

"Yes, it does!" Her voice rose. "People do things for a reason. Crimes aren't random. There are patterns."

"And you'll figure it all out." He slid both his hands over hers, cradling her trembling hands inside his palms. "But not right now. Right now, you need to relax and work with me to figure out how you're going to get out of this. Okay? We're going to think this out together."

Her shoulders relaxed and it was as if he could feel some of the tension slip from her limbs and into his. He leaned toward her and felt her forehead rest against his. He closed his eyes, and they stayed there for a second, their heads resting against each other and their faces so close that all he'd have to do was move an inch and their lips would meet. His voice grew gruff with emotions he couldn't even put into words. "You don't have to worry. I'm here. I've got you."

But what had him?

His heart was beating so sharply with every breath it was almost hurting him. He felt like he was standing on the edge of a cliff about to leap. It was more than sheer adrenaline. More than fear. No, whatever it was that now filled his aching chest was something he'd never felt on the battlefield. It felt like scrambling desperately for a parachute, just so he could give it away.

He opened his eyes and pulled back. But still his hand never left hers.

"So, you know an M67 is a fragmentation hand grenade," he said. "Modern. Very common."

"Round and smooth," she added. "Not bumpy like a pineapple."

He smiled despite himself. "Right."

"Filled with shrapnel?" she asked.

"Steel fragments, actually."

"And I'm guessing just chucking it into the bathtub and running away is not an option?"

"Not a safe one, no. It could blow a hole through the building or take down a wall. And no clean line of escape means the debris could catch us while we were trying to run away." His eyes searched the room. Then he closed them and weighed his options. There was nothing up here sturdy enough to take or absorb the explosion. Throwing the grenade out the window into busy downtown Toronto could result in the loss of innocent lives. If it detonated inside the apartment the falling debris could still kill people on the street outside.

Dear God, he prayed, *help me know what to do. Help me find a way.*

"Once the spoon is released what's the time to detonation?" Her voice dragged his attention back to his face.

"Four seconds," he said, and opened his eyes. "Maybe five. Depending on the fuse. So, compared to what we went through with the land mine this morning we have tons of time."

A wan smile crossed her lips.

"Remind me of the casualty radius? How big is the explosion?"

He blinked. There was something about her logical, "just the facts" directness he absolutely adored. "About forty-nine feet or fifteen meters."

"Okay, Ms. Facts. I have some questions for you," he said. "How long will it take police to arrive?"

"Seventeen minutes is the average response time in this area. Mostly because of traffic."

Ouch. "Water will help absorb the explosion. How do we get it to water?"

"It's a twenty-five-minute walk to Lake Ontario."

A twenty-five-minute walk through a busy street with a live hand grenade was a bad idea.

"Then here's what we do," he said. "I'll ease my hands away from yours and call the police on your cell phone. Then, while we're waiting for them to show up, we'll head downstairs to the parking lot. As much as I hate the idea of you having to carry a live grenade, we'll be more likely to survive if it detonates outside your apartment. Hopefully there'll be something like a rain barrel or some other container that will absorb some of the impact if we need to get rid of it fast. That okay by you?"

"Absolutely." Her eyes met his, firm and unflinching. "I've got this."

Something surged inside his chest. He almost would've kissed her. Instead, he pulled away from her slowly, inching his skin off hers, aware of every beat of her pulse under his fingers. He let go and she let out a long, slow breath, as if he'd been the only thing keeping her grounded and she was adjusting to gravity without him. Well, that made two of them.

He reached for the phone.

A voice snarled from the doorway. "Drop it right now and raise your hands! Or I'll shoot."

Samantha jumped. She spun toward the doorway, feeling the hand grenade almost slip from her fingers.

"Get down! Get down on the ground! Now!"

"Hey, man!" Joshua's voice was calm and steady. "Put the gun down. You don't want to do this."

She cradled the grenade to her chest and turned toward the door. It was the man with the square jaw and baseball cap. It was the snoop, the sneak, who'd tried to break into Olivia's computer, steal her tablet and trail them, and whose face had scowled at them from Yvonne's flyer. Now here he stood in her doorway, his face flushed with shouting and a gun clasped in both his hands. "You, lady! Drop that! Whatever that is! Hands up. Now!"

"I can't! It's a hand grenade." She tried to shout but could barely hear her own voice over his bellowing. For a moment, her mind filled with the memory of being gagged. Silenced. Her knees trembled, threatening to send her falling to the ground. She swallowed a breath so deep it stung her lungs and refused to let the fear win.

If she dropped that hand grenade, they would all die.

Help me God. With Your help, I will stay strong.

She could hear Joshua arguing with him, trying to calm him down, but he was struggling to even make himself heard, over the torrent of words. "Man, we're dealing with an explosive. She's holding a live hand grenade. Let us just call the authorities—"

"I am the authorities! And you're under arrest."

"Prove it. If you're really a cop, show us your badge and a warrant." The words flew from Samantha's mouth so automatically, her mind scrambled to catch up.

"My name is Detective Roy Davis!" He kept both hands on the gun. "And I don't need to show you ID. Now get down, hands up, or I will shoot you!"

Joshua's mouth set in a firm, grim line and she could tell in an instant he didn't much trust Roy.

"Listen! I'm holding a live hand grenade!" She stretched her hands out toward him, even knowing that half a room away he'd never be able to tell what she was holding. "I know it probably doesn't look like one. It was disguised as a Christmas ornament."

Roy's eyes flicked slightly. "Where did you get the explosive device?"

"It's an M67 grenade," Joshua said. "And if you really are who you claim to be you should back off and call the tactical unit."

"Not another word from you!" The so-called detective swung his gun toward Joshua. "Lady, where did you get the explosive device?"

"Someone put it on my Christmas tree. But—"

"Who told you it was an explosive device? Did he?"

"He didn't have to! I'm a fact-checker. I'm familiar with hand grenades!"

"Why is the front door broken?"

She pressed her lips together. It had been exactly like this when she'd been questioned by campus security about the break-in and assault in her dorm room. Barking questions at her. Impatient. Not listening. Making her feel stupid.

"I broke the door down!" Frustration filled Joshua's voice. "She was in danger and I was locked out. Now, I'll ask you again, show us your badge and call someone to come deal with this bomb."

Glee practically danced in Roy's eyes. What kind of detective was he? "Listen, creep, I know what you've done. You're going to pay."

"We don't have time for this!" Authority radiated through Joshua's voice. "Holster your weapon and let us get help, or I'll be forced to disarm you!"

A snarl curled on Roy's lip. He pointed the gun toward Joshua's leg. "Let's see how brave you are with only one knee cap."

Joshua rushed at Roy, catching him in the chest. For a moment, the men wrestled on the floor, fighting for control of the gun. Then Roy kicked out hard against the table, knocking the canoe off the base. A second kick and her tiny Christmas tree flew from its stand, spreading dirt across the floor. The gun fired. The cabinet shattered behind her.

She ran for the stairs clutching the grenade to her chest like a bird's egg.

Behind her she could hear the sounds of a struggle, the men fighting, voices shouting, the gun firing again and Joshua calling her name.

She didn't wait. Her feet pelted down the stairs.

She prayed to God for help. Help to get rid of the grenade without anybody getting hurt. What was she going to do?

She hit the second-floor landing and kept running. Her feet slipped on the worn carpet. She nearly fell as she hit the tiled entranceway, but she threw her weight sideways and landed hard on one knee, wincing in pain as she felt it bruise. She pulled herself up and kept running. The back door to the alleyway loomed ahead.

"Wait! Samantha! What's going on here?" Yvonne stepped out of her office, blocking her path.

They collided, knocking her landlady to the floor.

"I'm so sorry! Call nine-one-one. Tell them we've got an explosive!"

Her body pushed through the back door into the alley and froze, her brain desperately scanning the world around her. Sirens sounded in the distance but she couldn't tell if they were coming her way. To her right, voices babbled on the busy city streets. To her left, cars lined the narrow alley packed together like sardines.

A third gunshot split the air behind her, shattering the upstairs window. Falling glass rained down around her. She ran deeper into the alley. Her foot slipped on the slick ice.

She fell forward, landing in the slush on her hands and knees.

The grenade fell from her hand and landed in the snow.

Five seconds. She just had five seconds and then it would blow.

She crawled for it.

Four seconds.

Her fingers touched the cold metal orb. She gripped it with her fingertips.

Three seconds.

A hand grabbed her ankle from behind.

Two seconds.

She threw the grenade into the air. Watching it arc ahead of her even as she felt a second hand forcing her body down onto the slushy ground.

One.

The grenade landed in the Dumpster and exploded. She closed her eyes as the wall of snow, water and soggy debris rained down around her.

NINE

Samantha sat up on the hospital bed. Her brain felt fuzzy, and her mouth was dry. Her head throbbed in and out, making the narrow, blue-gray walls pulsate along with it. It had been like this in the hours after that guy had broken into her dorm room in college. Not being able to sleep but not being fully awake either. Knowing something had happened, but feeling like she'd just been sleepwalking through it. And now?

Come on, Samantha. Compile the facts and put them together in a logical order.

She was lying on a hospital bed in her own clothes. She'd run out of her apartment with the hand grenade. She'd been tackled by someone, hadn't she? Someone had grabbed her, but she'd never seen their face. She'd let the grenade fly. Then there'd been snow and slush exploding around her. Ringing in her ears. Darkness in her eyes. Then police officers in uniform helped her to her feet. Then an ambulance. Then a doctor. Kind hands checking her body, brushing the hair from her face, looking her in the eyes. Kind voices asking her serious questions about what she'd just seen and been through. But it was like she'd watched it all happen to someone else.

She'd cried out for Joshua. That she remembered. Searching everywhere for his face, asking everyone where he was.

And no one could tell her.

She heard footsteps on the other side of the curtain. They were heavy, like winter boots, instead of the soft-soled shoes the doctors and nurses wore. Then there was a gentle knock on the wall beside the hospital curtain. "Hello? Samantha?"

"Joshua!" She swung her feet over the edge of the bed.

The curtain drew back.

A roguishly handsome face with a trim beard and wet mop of hair. Gentle, kind eyes.

"No, sorry. Just me. I'm Alex. Joshua's friend? But you're not the first person to make that mistake."

Oh. The man of many talents who'd recently signed on as a bodyguard for Daniel's new security company. Guess that meant that she had a new bodyguard.

Alex stepped forward, tentatively, like he was afraid of spooking her. "Joshua called me from the police station and asked me to come get you. Nurse at the front desk told me that you were free to leave as soon as someone came to pick you up. Zoe's gone to the apartment to get your suitcase and see about getting your door and window replaced."

She was grateful. But somehow she felt too numb to even figure out how to express it properly. She was vaguely aware that Alex's words trailed off, like he was waiting for her to say something.

"Where's Joshua?" she asked. "Is he okay?"

Alex nodded. "He was taken in for questioning."

She could feel her heart rate pick up. She swung her legs over the side of the bed. "Do you mean he was arrested? Roy, or whatever his name is, never showed us his ID."

"My understanding is that Joshua voluntarily went with the police for questioning. I don't expect he'll be charged. I don't know who Roy is."

"Joshua might have attacked a detective."

"He did what?" Alex blinked.

"He was protecting me. Roy wasn't in uniform, didn't show a badge and wasn't listening. He pulled a gun on us. I had an explosive device in my hand." One that had turned out to be all too real. "Joshua saved my life."

She pressed the heels of her palms against the bed and stood. Almost instantly she felt woozy, like the world still hadn't come back into focus yet. Her knees wobbled. "What's wrong with me?"

"You're hungry, you're tired and you've gone through some pretty serious trauma." Alex stretched out his arm. "Come on, let's go meet up with Zoe, get you fed and get you back to the country house. Don't try to catch a train or make any major decisions until you've eaten and slept. You'll feel better in the morning. Joshua will be okay too. He knows how to take care of himself."

She let him help her to her feet. And only then realized his watch read quarter after four. "I never called Theresa."

"It's okay," Alex said. "I'm sure she'll understand and be willing to see you tomorrow. She's good that way. She's really good at helping people who've been through trauma."

But what if her brain and heart were both too broken to be fixed?

"Joshua told me you two used to be engaged?"

"We were." Alex looked down. She followed his gaze as they walked through the hospital hallway. His boots were making puddles of slush on the hospital floor. "A long time ago. She's extraordinary. But..." He shrugged. "Theresa would be the first one to tell you that liking someone, even loving them, isn't the same as figuring there's a way to make a life together."

Alex left her by the front door of the hospital and went to get the car. There was a coffee shop there. It was small, narrow and crowded. But still someone had taken the time to set up a small, intricately decorated Christmas tree on the counter, complete with tiny clay decorations, and to stencil snowflakes down the glass windows. There was something comforting about it. The idea that even in places that were chaotic, challenging and packed to the brim with worried, stressed-out people, Christmas still went on, in small, thoughtful, caring ways.

It was odd to think that tomorrow was Christmas Eve already. Usually, she'd be curled up at her parents' house by now, under a quilt, cracking nuts from the same wooden bowl they put out every year. Instead, she still hadn't made it to the train.

She didn't notice the curly-haired man in an expensive wool coat sitting at the tiny high table and playing on his cell phone, until he looked her way. Even then, she wasn't even sure Eric had actually seen her. But either way, the last thing she wanted was for him to look up and see her running out the door.

"Eric!" She raised her voice over the babble and waved a hand in his direction as she weaved her way through the coffee shop toward him.

He looked up.

"Samantha!" A wide smile crossed his boyish face. "What are you doing here?"

She stopped. She'd just assumed that he'd seen the chaos at the apartment building and come here looking for her. He stood up, scooping his cell phone back into his breast pocket. Then the handsome blue eyes that covered billboards from one side of the city to the other locked their full attention onto her. He reached for both her hands, held them out in front of her. "Are you all right? Are you hurt? Please tell me nothing happened to you."

Well, I found a live hand grenade in my apartment, and then some guy named Roy who claimed to be a detective ran in with a gun, and got into a fight with Joshua. Then I fell and the grenade went off...

"It's a very long story and I don't want to get into it right now. There was a major fight between a friend of mine and someone else back at my apartment that led to some damage. But actually I think I'm here because I slipped and fell on the ice."

"That's terrible." He squeezed both her hands together in one of his and despite the intended affection of the gesture, suddenly she remembered the feel of the bonds tying her wrists together. "I hate thinking about you being in this kind of danger. I have a spare room back at my apartment and a pretty decent live-in housekeeper if you're looking for a safe place. Or I can talk to my mother? Our relationship is tense. She's a bit clingy and I've had to distance myself from her some for the sake of my career, because otherwise she'd totally try to run my life. But I did tell her about you, and the gift to you was actually something she came up with."

So now he was suggesting she move in with him and his housekeeper, or maybe his clingy mother, who apparently also knew about her?

"Eric, thank you. But I'm going to stay with friends tonight and then head home to see my parents tomorrow. What are you doing here?"

"I'm worried about Bella. I think something bad might've happened to her."

"What?" Her neighbor from across the hall? The one who'd moved out and broken Eric's heart? "Why do you say that?"

"It never made sense that she'd just leave my life like that," he said. "She didn't tell me she wanted to break up. She just ghosted me and disappeared. You know I blamed myself and figured I'd done something to drive her away. But then you told me about the intruder in the building. What if he was stalking her? Or hurt her in some way? And then there's the letter she sent me after she left."

He pulled a piece of cream-colored printer paper out of his pocket and laid it down on the table. She looked down and read:

Dear Eric,
I don't want you in my life anymore.
This is goodbye forever. Please don't try
to find me. You're a wonderful man, and
I'm not good enough for you.
You're better off without me.
Bella

Samantha blinked. "What am I looking at?"

"Don't you see?" Eric's voice rose. "It's typed and printed on a sheet of computer paper. Anyone could've written this! I should've seen it earlier. Bella never would've sent me something like this!"

Wouldn't she? True, she hadn't known her neighbor well enough to know what she would or wouldn't write.

"When I was a teenager there was this girl I fell in love with in high school." Eric's words were spilling out so quickly she could barely keep up. "Then she moved away over the summer and sent me a letter saying she never wanted to see me again. She said the same thing, that I was really great and I was better off without her."

She was getting confused. Wasn't that the kind of thing people naturally said when they were trying to politely end a relationship? Eric had the tendency to babble. Sometimes she suspected he was popping caffeine pills and washing them down with energy drinks to manage the weird hours he kept due to working the early-morning show. He'd get all hyper and then he'd crash.

"What if there's a connection?" His voice rose. "Your newspaper ran a big story about a crime ring that was kidnapping teenaged girls. What if their disappearance is connected to that?"

Was it so unbelievable that a woman had broken up with him that he'd had to grasp at ridiculous straws? It was sad, and even worse than the time *Torchlight* had done a huge story on a disease breakout overseas and Eric had rushed over, convinced he was dying. Yes, she was familiar with the story of the gang who kidnapped teenage girls. She'd researched it. She also knew it had happened in a completely different part of the country and everyone involved had been arrested months ago.

"Eric, Bella told me she was moving and I saw the moving van myself. That crime ring was targeting girls much, much younger than Bella. You need to go home and get some sleep."

"I gave her a kitten as a present and it keeps coming back to you, like nobody's feeding it. So I called the police, but they had no record of anyone matching her description. So, next I thought I'd try the hospitals, but they didn't have any record of her either. You'd know stuff like that, right? You're a researcher."

Only what Eric was doing was the exact opposite of what she did. She looked at facts and figured out what they meant, even if that meant coming to conclusions she didn't much like. Eric had seized on the fact he couldn't have been rejected by a woman he cared about, invented and was twisting around every random fact he could find to make it true. The simplest answer was almost always the right one. It was far more likely Bella didn't want to date Eric anymore and that the cat had always roamed between multiple apartments getting fed.

Joshua had asked her if she thought Eric could have anything to do with what had happened to her. Honestly, she hadn't. Not only had her criminal research in the ATHENA database shown that Eric didn't have the pathology to plan something so nasty and devious, Eric seemed too needy for approval to hurt anyone. He was like an overgrown puppy. The idea he'd ever connive and scheme with common thugs to terrorize her seemed laughable. He wanted to protect Samantha, not hire creeps to blow her up.

Eric just didn't possess the cruel, calm, calculated evil needed to be Magpie.

Yet, at the same time she knew that if she'd been standing here in the hospital talking to any other friend, she'd have already offered to use her own contacts and research skills to help them confirm Bella was okay. In fact, she might just do that for her own peace of mind. It couldn't be that hard to do an internet search for her new address or to call around to moving companies just to confirm they had indeed moved a very live woman into a new home. Instead, Samantha couldn't shake the suspicion that if she did that she'd have been helping Eric stalk a woman who wanted nothing more than to be gone from his life.

A horn honked outside. Headlights flashed on and off.

"I've got to go," she said. "My ride is here. But I'll text you when I get back from Montreal and we'll have that coffee together. We need to sit down and talk."

"Just promise me you'll never disappear from my life without saying goodbye." His arms flew around her. He hugged her tightly and everything inside her body bristled. "Just don't, okay? I care about you and I want to protect you. I don't know what's wrong with me, that women I care about keep leaving me. I've got a lot of fans, but it's not the same. First my dad left, then my mom got really sad, and then the first girl I ever liked dumped me."

And sadly, if you keep smothering me like this, I'm going to need a break from you too.

The sky was dark, and heavy snow was pelting down by the time Joshua finally left the police station. He stopped outside the door under the protection of the overhang, squared his shoulders and looked out at the night. Well, that had been an exercise in utter futility. Roy, the so-called detective, had turned tail and run the moment police had shown up, which further solidified Samantha's suspicion that despite his firearm and penchant for spouting overused cop-show lingo, Roy definitely wasn't law enforcement.

So now we have an unstable snoop, posing as a detective, with an almost illegal firearm to add to our list of things to protect Samantha against.

If he was ever looking for an example of everything Gramps had been against when he railed about people just running around wildly with guns thinking they were authorities unto themselves, then Roy Davis, self-declared detective, was it.

But the police hadn't been interested in giving Joshua any answers either. Instead they just kept asking Joshua the same futile questions, over and over again, until he couldn't tell if they were trying to catch him up in a lie or couldn't think of anything to ask. Until, finally, he'd reminded them that he was there voluntarily and that if they were going to charge him with something that he really should call a lawyer. After that, it was amazing how quickly they told him he was welcome to leave.

A horn honked in the darkness. He started toward it. Alex's truck was sitting at the end of the parking lot with the engine idling. Joshua's rental car had been towed back to the rental agency after the rain of ice, snow and debris caused by the grenade explosion had left it with a cracked windshield and dented hood. He didn't even know if insurance covered explosives.

The snow was growing thicker by the moment.

"Hey, jailbird!" Alex rolled down the window. "I hope you're okay if we don't hang around the city much longer. I want to get on the highway before the weather gets too bad. It's supposed to dump a ton on us."

Joshua looked up at the sky. "Just promise me you're not going to crash this time."

"Ha ha." Alex grinned. "One day you're going to have to forgive me for that."

Joshua chuckled. Of course he'd forgiven Alex for crashing his very first truck. Didn't mean he had to stop teasing him about it, though. He'd already started around the side of the car before he realized that Samantha was in the passenger seat. Her sturdy suitcase sat by her feet beside her blue vintage hand-bag. She rolled the window down.

"You okay?" she asked.

He nodded, suddenly feeling emotion swell up in his chest, making it slightly hard to breathe. "Yeah, you?"

She nodded. "Yup. Thanks for reminding me to throw the grenade in water. The slush and snow in the Dumpster absorbed a lot of the blow."

The back door behind her seat swung open.

"Come on," Zoe said, leaning across the backseat. "Get in. Unless your feet are frozen to the pavement."

Something like that.

He climbed into the backseat. The front-seat windows rolled up. He shut the door and reached for his seat belt.

Then he looked up again. Three pairs of eyes were on his face.

"What now, boss?" Alex said.

Since when was he the boss? He'd just gotten out of a police station and he wasn't even an official part of this new private-security venture. It was hard enough trying to be a bodyguard without being voted de facto leader of what happened next.

He looked at Samantha. She'd turned around backward in the seat to face him.

"What's next for you?" he asked, softly.

"Well, my apartment's still standing, but I'm definitely going to take up Olivia's offer to stay at the country house tonight. Zoe and Alex helped me install a new door on my apartment and fix the window. Yvonne wasn't thrilled, but she was glad she didn't have to pay for it. So, I'm covered. You really do have the most extraordinary friends."

He grinned. "Yeah, I really do."

Alex put the truck in Drive and eased it through the parking lot.

"And how are you feeling?" Joshua asked her.

"The hospital gave me a clean bill of health," Samantha said. She turned back toward the window, so he was now looking at the back of her head. "I called Theresa and she's agreed to see me at ten tomorrow morning. Then I'll head to the train station right after that and hopefully catch an early-afternoon train to Montreal."

"Okay, sounds good." It was odd trying to have a conversation with the back of her head.

The truck merged with downtown traffic. Joshua closed his eyes and leaned back against the seat. Exhaustion seemed to seep into his bones. He wouldn't be surprised if he nodded off on the drive.

Samantha's sudden scream jerked him back to consciousness. A man's shape loomed large in the headlights. Alex hit the brakes, shouted to God for help and leaned into a skid as the truck spun into ongoing traffic. The blare of horns filled the air. Joshua felt Zoe grab his arm as her quiet prayers mingled with her brother's loud ones. The truck stopped, facing the wrong way on the crowded city street.

"Thank You, God, I didn't hit anyone!" Alex looked up at the roof and said a final prayer. Then he glanced back. "Sorry about that, guys. Apparently I was getting more of an opportunity than I expected to demonstrate my stellar driving skills."

Joshua leaned forward. "What happened?"

"Some lunatic leaped right out in front of the car and waved his hands like an air-traffic controller. Some of the people in this city are crazy. I'm just really, really thankful I didn't crash and nobody was hurt."

Joshua looked out the window. Pedestrians were crowding around. Horns were honking. Other vehicles seemed more intent on squeezing around them than actually stopping long enough to let Alex move.

"Do you want me to get out and direct traffic while you try to turn around?" Samantha asked, beating Joshua to the question that was on the tip of his tongue.

"Thanks, but not yet," Alex said. He checked his blind spot. "Hopefully the light will change in a moment and the traffic will clear."

"Hey!" Suddenly two fists were banging on the hood, again and again, hard and relentless. It was Roy. "I see you in there! I know what you did! And you're not going to get away with it!"

TEN

"Jessica Wynne from Huntsville!" The so-called detective pounded on the truck again, like he was on a televised cop drama and the hood was his interrogation-room table. "Holly Williams from Ottawa! Isobel Joyner from Mississauga! Monique Nash from Windsor!"

"Does that mean anything to you?" Samantha glanced back at Joshua. "Heard any of those names before?"

"No. I haven't."

Clearly Samantha hadn't either. But here the man was, shouting them over and over again, like he thought they should mean something. Joshua opened the car door, even as he could hear Alex yelling at him not to do anything foolish. But if that man pulled a weapon on a crowded city street, a lot of innocent people could get hurt if Joshua wasn't there to disarm him.

"I don't know who those women are."

Joshua stepped out into the snow. "And I'm pretty sure you're no detective."

Roy stopped. He walked around the truck slowly, his eyes locked on Joshua. In the corner of his mind, Joshua was keenly aware of the crowd of pedestrians on the sidewalks, the vehicles trying to creep around them, the police station only two blocks away and the lives of three people he cared about sitting between them in the vehicle. But he locked all of his attention on the angry red face of the man slowly pacing him around the vehicle.

"You know what you've done," Roy said.

"Are you sure about that?" Joshua asked. "Because, like I said, I've never heard of those women and I've never heard of you. So whatever vendetta you think you're chasing down, and whoever you're chasing it for, it has nothing to do with me."

But could it have anything to do with the threats against Samantha?

Roy hesitated. His hand reached inside his jacket pocket. Joshua braced himself and prepared to rush him. Sirens sounded in the distance. Roy turned on his heels and ran, dodging through traffic. Joshua started after him. The lights changed, vehicles started moving again, a car cut across his path and

Joshua was barely able to stop as it came within a breath of hitting him.

"Joshua! Come on!" Alex shouted.

He looked back. Alex had inched the truck around until it was creeping up the road behind him. He paused, torn. Roy had disappeared in the crowd ahead of him, in a busy downtown street with dozens of doors and hundreds of escape points. There was no way to know for sure where he'd gone. Meanwhile, his friends sat in the truck behind him. Police were running toward them from the side. He gritted his teeth. He'd promised to protect Samantha. To be her bodyguard. He could hardly do that and go on a wild-goose chase through the darkened city streets. His eyes rose to the thickly falling snow.

Help me, God. I don't know what I'm supposed to be doing here.

He walked back to the truck. He looked at Samantha, but her head was bowed. Her fingers moved quickly over the tablet screen.

"Zoe's on the phone with police," Alex said as Joshua hopped in. "I'm not sure if they're going to want to interview us for long, considering he didn't pull a weapon, nobody got hurt and I'm not sure what they'd even charge him with. But I'm going to pull back around and park at the police station again."

Alex inched forward. Traffic barely moved around them.

"Do you know what that was about?" Alex asked.

"No clue. I don't even know what he was saying."

"He was listing off women's names," Samantha said. She didn't look up. "Jessica Wynne from Huntsville. Isobel Joyner from Mississauga or Markham, something like that. Holly someone…"

"Williams." Zoe hung up the phone. "Holly Williams. Ottawa."

Samantha nodded. "The other was a Nash and all I can remember is she was from somewhere else in Ontario."

"Windsor," Joshua said quietly.

"Thanks. Monique Nash from Windsor." Samantha went back to typing. He'd never seen anyone's fingers move so fast. "I'm guessing there's a good Wi-Fi signal back at the country house?"

He nodded. "There is. Why, what are you doing?"

This time she looked up. Her eyes met his in the rearview mirror. "My job. Because whether he meant to or not, that unstable man just gave me the one thing I've been need-ing—names. Maybe one of those women is

Magpie. Maybe they're all working for Magpie. Or maybe Roy is." She looked back down at the tablet. "If any of those names, or Roy, are connected to *Torchlight News* in any way, or a bigger pattern of unsolved crimes, or anything else I can put a finger on, I'm going to find out."

Beating snow buffeted hard against the country house window. A fire crackled softly in the fireplace. Joshua turned and looked out at the darkness through the fresh pane of glass Alex and Zoe had installed, but saw nothing but the reflection of his own face ringed in the light of the fire behind him and dozens of dots of sparkling light from the Christmas tree. Samantha sat behind him, curled up sideways in an armchair by the fire. Two blankets were wrapped around her, one around her feet and one around her shoulders.

Zoe's dog, Oz, whimpered at the bottom of the chair for a moment, until Samantha absentmindedly reached down, scooped him up and dropped him into the crook of her knees. He curled into a tiny ball and promptly fell asleep.

"If you think that dog's sweet now," Joshua said, "you should see him when Alex gets out his keyboard and tries to play Christmas carols. Oz howls."

"Cute." A smile crossed her lips. She laughed under her breath and rubbed the dog's head. Then she went back to typing. It had been over an hour since they'd gotten back to the country house and she hadn't let go of the tablet once. Not even while she called Olivia to talk about Magpie's outrageous demand that *Torchlight* delete their entire ATHENA database. Even though Alex and Zoe had wandered off to other parts of the sprawling house, something had kept him rooted here, in this room, next to Samantha, watching her work. Gone was the uncertainty and helplessness he'd seen in her just hours ago. Now it had been replaced with a new drive, a fire in her eyes, a focus. It had taken twice as long to get back to the country house as it had to get downtown in the morning. And of course, they'd had a trip to the police station that had been longer than predicted.

The snow had been so bad by the time they'd left the city limits they'd stopped at a rest stop after an hour to refill the windshield wiper fluid and grab greasy hamburgers for a quick dinner. And the whole time, Samantha's tablet had barely left her hands.

She looked up, as if sensing her eyes on

him. The lights of the Christmas tree behind
her seemed to illuminate the lines of her form
like a hundred tiny spotlights. Her deep, dark
gaze looked through him. Her lips parted.
His heart struck a hard beat in his chest. For
a moment he thought she was about to speak.
But instead, she frowned and looked back
down at the tablet. Within seconds the typing had started up again. He nearly laughed.
Even scowling at the screen she was beautiful. It was almost unreal. Like she was an
old-fashioned starlet who'd slipped off the silver screen somehow and into the quiet space
where he sat. Someone Gramps might have
admired. Or might have warned him about.

What would Gramps have thought of Samantha, if he were still alive? More impor-
tantly, what would Dad now think if Joshua
brought a woman like her home? The weird-
est thing about the whole day was that normally he, Alex and Zoe were such a tight
group that adding a new person into the mix
was jarring. Even Theresa had always felt like
an outsider. But there was something comforting about Samantha. She was quirky, for
sure, but somehow she fit. He'd always taken
it for granted that being in a relationship with
a woman meant dealing with the never-end-
ing chatter and demands of someone con-

stantly needing his attention. Now, for the first time, he could imagine the comfortable, comforting silence of two hearts just beating side by side. He'd never expected to meet someone this captivating in real life. Somehow he suspected that no matter how old he lived to be, he never would again.

Even if another man had told him today that he was going to marry Samantha. Joshua needed to come clean with her about that. And get more than a few questions answered. But it wasn't like he'd been about to question her about Eric during the day she'd had.

But now, what was his excuse? How focused she looked? Or how, even though he was nearly positive Eric was greatly exaggerating the nature of their relationship to the point of outright lying, he didn't want to interrupt the most peaceful, comfortable moment she may have had in a long time?

It wasn't like he was in any position to pursue a relationship with her. If he reenlisted for another nine-year term of front-line service overseas, what kind of life would that be for her? Did he really want to repeat the same mistake Gramps had made? But if he turned down a good job with a pension just because he didn't much like it, then he had no business trying to be the husband of a woman like her anyway.

Samantha sighed loudly. Her hands shot up to the ceiling. Then she rolled her shoulders around in a circle.

"You all right?" he asked. "Were you able to find anything?"

She blinked as if the question had jolted her back from wherever her head had been. Her eyes met his. She smiled self-consciously. "Oh, I've found plenty. So very much, in fact. But nothing helpful. None of it makes any sense or seems to fit together in any logical way."

She shifted her legs and leaned forward, turning the tablet toward him. A chart of some sort filled the screen, with boxes of texts and pictures. It was like staring at the electronic version of a police crime board.

"The first woman Roy mentioned, Jessica Wynne from Huntsville, died two years ago. She was hit by a car after leaving the gym where she worked as a boxing instructor. Holly Williams from Ottawa disappeared over a decade ago after going kayaking alone. Police assume she drowned. She was only sixteen. Both Jessica and Holly were athletic, and both deaths were declared accidents. But there's almost eight years between

their deaths and nothing obvious to connect
them. Monique Nash was shot dead leaving
the coffee shop where she worked, six years
ago. I found police reports and news stories
on all three. Monique's death was already in
ATHENA database because she was refer-
enced in an article on gun crime. Usually if
this was the work of a serial killer there'd be
some kind of pattern. Here there's no pattern."

He felt his jaw drop. *She called this finding nothing helpful?* He'd gone on missions
with less information than that.

"I can't find anything on Isobel Joyner at
all. No police report. No news stories. So,
if she is dead too, from either an accident
or murder, it never made the press. But, I
did figure out a whole bunch about our new
buddy, Detective Roy." She tapped a square
at the corner of the tablet's screen, and a website opened up. "Private Detective Roy Davis.
Based just outside Toronto. Fired from the
police services years ago for aggressive tendencies. Fired from a private security job
shortly afterwards for punching a coworker.
Nasty piece of work and get this…" Her fingers moved again, and suddenly he was looking at some kind of social media page. "He's

been bragging online for weeks about being hired to track down a serial killer."

"What?" Somebody hired him to run around with his gun making wild threats and accusations? He groaned. People like that gave cops like his dad a bad name and caused more problems than they solved. "Well, considering he definitely wouldn't even qualify for a Canadian permit to carry that handgun he threatened us with, it shouldn't take much for police to arrest and charge this guy."

He ran his hand along his jaw.

"What does this have to do with Magpie or anything that's happened to you in the past twenty-four hours?"

"I don't know. That's the whole point. I can't see anything connecting any of this to anything else." She picked the tablet up and opened it back up to the first screen she'd showed him. Then she zoomed out. He let out a long breath. The chart was at least three times larger than he'd seen at first, and it was all there: a complete step-by-step time line of everything that had happened since he'd first found her tied up on the front porch, every one of Magpie's warnings, every person they'd run into, every incident, all laid out in one big, comprehensive fact tapestry.

He was impressed.

"You made this?" He didn't even try to conceal the awe in his voice.

"Yes, and it makes no sense," she said. "If this story landed on my desk as some big investigative piece I'd bounce it back to the reporter in an instant for not making his case."

Her voice rose.

"There should be connections!" Her finger slid through the air above the screen. "Ways in which A connects to B connects to C. One central story. A big picture. Like, 'Torchlight News fact-checker Samantha Colt was kidnapped and threatened by so-and-so, because of such-and-such, which could be linked to the death and disappearance of four other Canadian women by XYZ.' There's nothing here to imply these four women are even connected, let alone to explain why Roy's investigation led to him skulking both around my apartment and my work, and why something called Magpie keeps threatening my life. This is wild-goose-hunt journalism at its worst, trying to tenuously tie a bunch of random, disconnected terrible things together, with nothing connecting them other than the fact that I'm somehow caught in the middle of it."

"Maybe Roy Davis is unhinged and it's just a coincidence he showed up," Joshua said. "Maybe Roy and these women have nothing to do with Magpie. If I've learned anything on the battlefield, it's that sometimes very bad things just happen and we'll never find out why."

"Or maybe there is a connection but it's locked in my head and I can't remember it." She pressed her hands against her eyes. "I feel so useless."

"Are you kidding me?" He crossed the space between them in two steps and picked up the tablet. "Look at everything you've done. None of this is anything you should feel the slightest bit sorry for."

"Yes, it kind of is." Her hands dropped into her lap and he could see the shine of tears in the corners of her eyes. "Because if I could remember how I got from the alley to the van then maybe we'd know something. Maybe we'd have some answers and my editor—who's just had a baby—and the rest of the senior staff wouldn't be having an emergency meeting about the fact some maniac is demanding we delete our whole news database. But we still don't have any idea who this Magpie is or what game they're playing, because of me."

"Don't say that." Joshua dropped down to his knees in front of her chair. He set the tablet down carefully on the table, then took both her hands in his. "None of this is your fault. None."

"You keep saying that."

"Yeah, and I'm going to keep saying it until you start to hear me and believe it." He squeezed her hands tightly. "Not only are none of the crimes you've lived through in the past twenty-four hours your fault, but you've handled them with so much courage and so bravely that it impressed me. I'm a *soldier*. I've seen countless people fall apart in the battlefield because they didn't have half your brains and guts under fire. The fact you don't remember the details of how you were kidnapped doesn't weaken you. In fact, it's very normal."

Her head was still shaking. "But what if I never remember anything helpful? Ever? What if Magpie keeps threatening people and my newspaper is forced out of business? When I could've stopped that from happening if I'd just figured out the final piece of the puzzle. What if I sit down to talk to Theresa tomorrow and completely fail to remember anything more than what I already know?"

"I get that figuring out facts is your job," he said. *Just like protecting people is mine.* "But even if you don't remember any new facts that will help the police and your employers sort out this mess, that doesn't mean you've failed." He pulled one of his hands away from hers. He wiped the back of his fingers across her cheek, feeling the wetness of her tears. "Tomorrow's appointment is about helping you, giving you peace of mind and helping you heal. I promise you that no matter what happens, no matter what you do or don't remember, I'll still be proud of you."

"Thank you." Tears danced on her lashes. She leaned toward him. Her face fell into the cup of his hand and he felt the delicate curve of her cheek against his fingers. "You're a good friend and a wonderful bodyguard."

His fingers brushed the soft hair beside her cheek. His rib cage tightened around his heart.

He felt like a fraud. Because all he wanted to do now was to kiss her. To pull her into his arms and hold her close to his chest so she could feel his heart against hers. To utterly destroy everyone who had ever tried to hurt her. To throw his own life between hers and danger.

And I can't trust a single thing I'm feeling right now is real or going to last. Because my heart's never beat this way before.

"Thank you." His words sounded awkward to his own ears, as if something was pressing up against his lungs. He pulled away, stood up quickly and picked up the tablet again. "Is your friend Eric Gibson on this chart?"

"No." She stood slowly, managing to slide her body off the chair without sending Oz tumbling to the floor. "But I did put his ex-girlfriend Bella on the chart. He was pretty panicked about her today, wondering why Bella had moved out without saying good-bye in person and hoping she wasn't in trouble. He gets that way sometimes and it takes a while to talk him down. I think he takes some kind of caffeine stimulant to get through the morning show and it's not good for his brain and his emotions. Also, I don't think he's very good at rejections." She ran both hands through her hair. "Bella sent him a break-up letter. She told me she was moving out and she asked me about hiring a moving company. Then, a few days later, a moving van shows up and moves all her stuff out. Yvonne complained that she ran out on her rent and her security deposit won't cover the damage. But considering how Yvonne can be I can't exactly fault Bella for breaking her lease. It's wrong, but understandable, and it doesn't sound anything like foul play to me. But Eric was worried about it, plus Roy was snooping around the building, so I added it.

Just in case it has anything to do with anything. Not that I can tell what actually has anything to do with anything anymore. And Eric's been acting...odd."

An understatement. Given his conversation with Eric earlier, Joshua still had his reservations.

She yawned deeply, then turned to the study door by the Christmas tree. "I think I'm going to go lie down. I know it's only eight. But my head's swimming. Maybe if I close my eyes for fifteen minutes this will all make more sense."

"You're welcome to rest in my room upstairs. I'll take the study."

"No, thank you, but it's fine. My suitcase is in there already."

She reached up. Her hand brushed his shoulder and for a moment it seemed like she was about to pull him in for a hug.

"Eric told me he's planning on marrying you," he said.

"Really? He did?" She let go and blinked. "He did warn me he'd said something outrageous to you that he regretted. But I'd never realized it was that. I'm guessing he lied to make you think I had someone looking out for me. Believe me, I don't have any intention of marrying him."

She turned and started for the office.

"But that's quite a statement, isn't it? You've never been romantically involved with him?"

He winced as the awkward words left his lips. He must sound ridiculous, like some crush-struck youth inquiring whether he had a rival.

"No, of course not." She stopped and turned back. "Eric is emotionally clingy and very protective. He tries too hard to be my friend. Maybe he has a crush on me. I think he's still in love with Bella, but he does seem like the kind of man to have feelings for two women at once. But that doesn't justify him saying something so completely untrue. Even though he'll probably apologize for it again later by saying that he was only trying to protect me. He seems determined to stick around in my life for the long term."

She stood there for a long moment, her hand on the door to the study. Silence crackled between them like kindling in the fire, filled with words neither of them were willing to say. Then a sigh left her lips. "See you in a bit."

The door closed firmly behind her.

Night fell deeper. The snow grew heavier, until it was coming down so thick and fast that he worried about how long it was going to take to dig out the car in the morning. He had cocoa in the kitchen with his friends. Then Alex and Zoe went upstairs to bed. Joshua stretched out on the full length of the couch in the living room, not quite ready to go upstairs to bed yet. His eyes ran toward the closed study door. Samantha still hadn't stirred. Hopefully that meant she was getting the sleep she needed. His watch beeped midnight.

Christmas Eve had arrived.

He pulled off his watch, dropped it on the table, and draped the blankets over his body. He took a deep breath and felt his racing heart slow in his chest.

Thank You, God, for bringing us all again safely through to the end of the day. Please guide and equip us for whatever the next day brings when the sun rises again.

Joshua didn't remember falling asleep or even saying Amen. But suddenly he was awake. The clock read four thirty in the morning.

And Samantha was screaming in terror.

ELEVEN

She was back in her college dorm room. She was nineteen. She was terrified. There was someone there, pushing her down. His hand clamped to her mouth. The other hand was clamped on her throat. And all Samantha could hear was the echo of her own panicked screams filling her ears, somehow screaming with no voice. As she kicked and hit and thrashed out against her attacker.

"Samantha! Are you all right? Open the door!"

Someone was shouting her name. She sat up. The room was dark. The springs were firm beneath her. She was on a sofa bed. Cushions cascaded down off the back around her. She had no idea where she was.

All she knew was he was going to hurt her unless she found a way to stop him.

A door flew open ahead of her. A man stood there. He was nothing but a silhouette, dark and huge in the night. He was blocking the doorway, blocking her way to freedom. Not this time. He wouldn't hurt her this time. This time she would fight. She would run.

Her hand slid down feeling for the heavy flashlight she'd kept beside her bed. Instead, the handle of her hard suitcase touched her fingers. She clenched it hard. The man stepped into the room. She leaped up and swung, striking him hard in the chest with the case, using it to battle her way to freedom.

She could still hear her voice. Filling the night. Filling the air. Screaming and screaming and screaming and she couldn't stop.

"Samantha! It's okay. It's me. Stop!"

He yanked the suitcase from her hand. She shoved past him and ran out into the living room. Fumbling in the dark she found a door. Her fingers struggled with the door locks. She yanked back the bolt.

"Josh!" a second male voice shouted. "Everything all right?"

"Alex! Josh! What's going on?" A female voice joined in.

"I don't know. I just woke up and she was screaming. Alex, check the perimeter and make sure we don't have a break-in. Zoe, check the inside of the house—"

The last latch flew back. Samantha threw

herself out into the night. She tumbled across rough, uneven boards on the front porch then pitched forward down a flight of stairs. She landed on her hands and knees, crawled forward. Cold stung her bare hands and seeped through her socks. She couldn't breathe. She couldn't see. She couldn't feel anything but the cold and dark and freezing cold seeping into her limbs. Then fresh snow was falling on her head. She stumbled to her feet and started running. Cold air stole her breath from her lungs. Her voice felt hoarse.

"Samantha!" A man was shouting her name now. It was a strong voice, a sturdy voice. A voice that spoke of safety and home. "It's okay. You're okay. Nobody's going to hurt you."

She woke up as the nightmare fled from her mind.

Darkness and snow filled her eyes.

She was outside. How had she gotten outside?

She sank to her knees, her frozen limbs giving way.

Tears filled her eyes. She was lost. She was cold. She was alone. Again.

"Samantha. Hey." Joshua's strong body dropped down onto his knees in the snow in front of her. His warm hands cupped her face. Tender lips brushed the cold tears from her cheek. Then gently his mouth moved over hers, and the hot breath of his kiss seemed to bring life back into her frozen lungs. A deep voice spoke in her ear, filling her heart with warmth. "It's okay. I'm here. You're safe. I'm not going to let anything happen to you."

"Joshua." A sob choked her throat. "Thank you." She fell forward into the strength and warmth of his chest, letting him curl his arms around her.

He gathered her into his arms and stood, lifting her from the snow and cradling her to his chest. "It's okay. I've got you."

The fear and fight left her body. Her head dropped against his shoulder.

"Are you okay?" His hand brushed her face. "What happened?"

The night terrors. The night terrors are back. The screaming in the night. The leaping out of bed and running away in terror until I wake up and don't even know at first where I am. The nightmares that suddenly feel so terrifying and so strong they take over and I can't tell nightmare from reality.

"Sweetheart, please." He ran one hand over the back of her head, protecting her from the falling snow. "What happened?"

"There was a guy who lived on the same

floor as I did." Her voice came out in a whisper. "I didn't really know him. He burst into my room and he pushed me down." She swallowed hard. "He attacked me. So I hit him. I hit him and kicked him as hard as I could until he let go. And then I ran and ran and ran."

His voice sounded pained, like somehow her words were making it hard for him to breathe. "Right now? Tonight?"

She shook her head, feeling tears course down her cheeks. "A very long time ago. But sometimes in the night I'm dreaming it's happening again."

He nodded, like he understood without saying a word. Then he unzipped his jacket, and she could feel his heartbeat as strongly as if it were inside her body. Joshua carried her through the snow back to the house, cradling her against his chest, and for once she was too tired to fight his protection. She was tired of running. She was tired of fighting the same fight, over and over and over again in her sleep, and never being able to win. She was tired of fighting against memories that came up in the depths of the night, but which her daylight mind didn't know how to piece together.

So instead, she laid her head against his

chest, listened to the crunch of snow under his boots, and let the words flow from her lips. She told him about the memories that suddenly appeared in the middle of the night without warning—waking her, shaking her, sending her running out into the night, screaming—as the darkness and the snow swirled around her. Memories that were ready to be put into words, in a way she'd never been ready to talk about them before.

"I told you some about what happened back when I was in college."

"Mmm-hmm," he murmured. It was the kind of comforting sound that said he was there and that he was listening. How could he sound so calm? She'd just dragged him out screaming into the middle of a snowstorm.

"I lived in this huge dorm building with hundreds of other people. I hated it. Even in my own room I could hear everything else going on. I never had any peace and quiet. There was a lot of late-night partying. One night, one of the guys on my floor mixed some illegal drugs with alcohol and went on a rampage, running around, vandalizing stuff, breaking things..."

Joshua stopped walking. She could feel the muscles in his neck strain, as he turned his head one way and then the other. She raised her head to look for the house, but all she could see was the darkness. "We're lost, aren't we?"

"Don't worry," he said. "Keep talking. Let me worry about finding the house."

"But, I should be helping. I caused this mess."

She started to slip from his arms. But he tightened his grip around her and held her close.

"No, let me carry you. You're not wearing shoes and you're not dressed for this weather. The last thing either of us needs is for you to get hypothermia." He adjusted his grip, lifting her higher. "Plus as long as I'm holding you, and we're sharing my jacket, your body warmth is keeping me warm." Then he started walking again. "And keep talking. Tell me your story. It helps me focus."

She wasn't sure how it could possibly help. But she could feel fear beginning to curl around the edges of her mind. The storm was vicious. If they didn't find the house they could freeze.

"People called campus security. I called campus security. But they told me he'd just run around drunk, tire himself out and pass out. Maybe I didn't explain the situation right. Maybe they didn't understand what I was trying to tell them. But eventually they told me to grow up and hung up. I remember lying in my tiny bed, in my little dorm room, hearing this guy stomping around the hallway, trying to ignore it and pretend it wasn't happening."

Again, Joshua paused. Fear was rising higher in her throat. Blocking out her memories. Blocking out her words. Blocking out everything except fear. And guilt. She was the reason they were in this danger. She was the reason they were in the cold. She was the reason all of this was happening. It was all her fault.

"Keep talking." His voice was gentle but firm. His lips brushed her freezing cheek. "Please."

"This wasn't the first time something like this happened. It was a party college. People got drunk and ran around at night like idiots all the time. I hated it."

A light flickered in the distance. Once again, Joshua stopped. Her breath caught in her chest. The light disappeared again. Swallowed up in the snow. She could feel his chest tighten beneath hers.

He started jogging.

Lord, help us! Direct him! Guide his steps.

"Keep talking." There was an edge to his

voice now. An urgency. As if the story, her terrible story, was all that was keeping them alive.

"I took half a sleeping pill. Nothing major. Just something my doctor had prescribed because sometimes I was so stressed about studying that my brain kept me up and I couldn't relax." Her teeth were chattering so badly she could barely speak. "Here's where the memory gets blurry. I remember lying down on my bed. I remember banging. Then I remember him standing in the open doorway of my dorm. I don't know how he got the door open. I don't know if I left it open, or he knocked and I let him in, or if he broke in somehow. All I know is somehow then he was on top of me. Choking me. Pushing me down. One hand on my throat so I couldn't breathe. And I hit him. I hit him and hit him and hit him, and kicked and thrashed and fought until he let go and I ran."

And that's all I know. And I've never stopped running since.

"I'm so sorry." He hugged her tightly.

Then he stopped walking again. The wind howled.

"Alex! Zoe! If you can hear me get in the car and honk the horn!" he shouted. But his voice was swallowed up in the whistle of cold wind surrounding them, whipping around them. She wasn't sure how far they'd strayed from the porch. The wind whistled. It hissed. It roared. The whiteout blurred the world around them.

God, please help me. Pleas for help welled up inside Joshua's heart as he stared out at the darkness blurring around him. If only the light would stay steady. But he'd see it for a second and run with all his might toward it. Only to then have it swallowed up in the snow again.

Samantha's words had fallen silent. Because she'd reached the end of the story? Or because she was too cold and exhausted to keep talking?

He had to stay strong for her. He should've thought before he ran out after her into the storm. She'd gotten farther than he'd imagined. He should've planned. He should've remembered just how easy it would be to get lost outside in a storm on a night like this, like settlers who were found dead just steps from their barn. Instead he'd just grabbed his coat and gone running out after her into the night.

He could feel Samantha shifting. He was aching to rest. His arms shook from her weight, the cold and from fatigue.

Help me, God. Help me see what I need to see. Give me the strength to carry on.

A disjointed sound floated on the air. Music? Then a piercing, shrill howling overtook the air. *Oz!* That blasted dog had a piercing voice that was sharp enough to cut through anything, even a storm.

"Hang on," he said. "And don't let go."

He felt her arms slip around his neck and hold him so tightly it almost hurt. A smile crossed his lips. "We're almost home."

He pelted through the snow toward the barking, forcing his legs past the point of exhaustion, past the point of pain, past the point of his even being able to feel them. He ran toward the barking, and the light that appeared and disappeared in the darkness, until he could hear the sound of music playing and Zoe shouting his name. He felt the rough gravel of the driveway under his feet and saw Zoe's pale face through the open back door.

"Josh!" Relief filled Zoe's voice. "Samantha! Oh, thank You, God!"

He tumbled into the kitchen and onto the hardwood floor, barely managing to set Samantha down safely before collapsing. Zoe flung the door closed behind them and bolted it. The music stopped.

Alex ran in from the living room. "We've

got to warm them up. Can you heat up a drink? Warm, not hot. Then we've got to get them something dry to change into."

"On it."

Alex knelt and draped a blanket over Samantha. He reached to drop a second one around Joshua, but Joshua shrugged it off and pushed the second one onto Samantha, as well.

"Come on, man, work with me here." Alex knelt beside him. Carefully, his hands checked Samantha's hands and feet for exposure. But his worried eyes kept glancing to his friend's face. "There's no use you saving her, if you're then too sick to be any good to us, now, is there?"

Another blanket landed heavy on his shoulders and this time he didn't fight. He could feel the world spinning. He was going to pass out, here on the floor with Samantha's body leaning up against him, her head on his shoulder, his arm around her waist. Oz crawled into their laps, trying to stretch his tiny body between them. Zoe pushed a mug into Joshua's hands. He chugged. His throat burned.

"Steady there," Alex said. "You should sip, not gulp."

For a moment the kitchen was a flurry of soft voices and gentle movements, as his friends hovered around him and Samantha like protective warriors around fallen comrades. Then Zoe ran off to draw hot water upstairs, while Alex disappeared to find clothes, and Joshua found himself alone with Samantha in the kitchen.

Samantha's head nestled into the crook of his neck. Her hand clenched the front of his shirt, her fingers curling around the fabric as if she was afraid of ever letting him go. And it was as if something inside his chest burst like a dam of emotions he'd been holding back for too long. How was it possible to feel so much for someone he'd just met? He didn't know. But it was like she'd crawled inside his chest and made his heart her home.

His lips brushed slowly over the top of her head. She turned toward him and looked up into his eyes with a look filled with a trust so deep he ached to be worthy of it.

"You found me," she whispered. "I was so lost…"

Her words trailed off, and he kissed her before she could find them again. His hands tightened around her. Her hands slid up around his neck. And for a half a second they clung to each other like two shipwrecked survivors.

Then, before the kiss could deepen, he

heard the gentle creek of his friends' approaching footsteps on the floorboards. He pulled back and let go.

Zoe cleared her throat. "Hot water's ready if you are."

Samantha nodded. "Thank you."

She stood slowly and let Zoe lead her upstairs.

Alex was leaning on the door frame, his face grave. Had Alex seen the kiss? Had Zoe? Joshua unwound his limbs from the tangle of blankets on the floor.

"We checked inside the house and out," Alex said as he reached for Joshua's hand and helped him to his feet. "We didn't find evidence of any intruders."

Joshua watched as Samantha disappeared up the stairs. "I don't think you will."

They walked through to the living room. His khaki sweatshirt and a fresh pair of jeans lay on a chair near the door. Alex tossed them to him without really making eye contact. "Here, pulled this from the dryer."

"Thank you." He stepped around the open door into the study and changed quickly. The room where Samantha had been sleeping looked like it had been the scene of some kind of battle. The blankets she'd been sleeping under were tossed on the floor. Her suitcase lay on its side, its contents strewn from where she'd hit him with it.

"Samantha's in better shape than you are." Alex's voice wafted through a crack in the door. "I figure she was only out there a couple of minutes before you got to her. Could've been a lot worse."

"She had a night terror." Joshua walked back into the living room, thankful for the warmth of dry clothes against his skin. "I'm not going to pretend to be a psychologist. But I've served with guys who'd start screaming, or running, or even going for their weapons in the night. They said it feels more like a flash-back in your sleep than a normal nightmare."

"Theresa will be able to help her with that." Alex walked over to the fireplace. He knelt and began to slowly coax the dead fire back to life.

"I hope so."

"And how are you?"

Joshua dropped into a chair. "I'm fine."

"No, you're not." Alex looked up at him. Already Joshua could hear the quiet crackle of growing flames. "I saw the look on your face when you ran out into the snow after Samantha. I've never seen you so panicked. And then the look on your face when you carried her in, and the way you kissed her…"

Alex waved his hands and shook his head, as if even putting what he'd seen into words failed him. "You've got some pretty heavy-duty emotional thing going on for Samantha, and that's not like you. How are you even feeling right now?"

Falling for a woman is like getting sick, Gramps used to say. *It's like a disease that just hits you all of a sudden, and she's the only medicine. But the more medicine you take, the sicker you get.*

Well, Gramps might've been wrong on that one. Because whatever this feeling was, it felt nothing like being sick. In fact, it was like the opposite of that. It was like being healthier and stronger than he'd ever been before, because there was someone else who needed him.

"To be honest, I have no idea what I'm feeling," Joshua said. How had he just lost his head and kissed her like that? "But what I'm *thinking* is that Samantha is catching a train home in a few hours tomorrow, and we still have no idea why anyone is out to hurt her. I've only got three more days before I have to report back to base, and I still haven't decided what I'm going to do about reenlisting. I don't want to reenlist. But I feel like I'd be letting my grandfather's memory down if I don't."

Alex nodded. It was the kind of nod that said something was bothering him and he wasn't sure whether or not he should say it. He stood slowly.

"You know Samantha has another man in her life?" Alex asked. "Eric Gibson, the Silver Media radio host?"

"I did. How did you?"

"I saw him hugging her at the hospital and recognized him from his billboard."

"She says he's just a friend, but I get the impression it's a pretty lopsided friendship. He seems really persistent and determined to be in her life, even though she finds him a bit much. But she told me not to worry about it."

Alex's eyes glanced to the empty doorway, and suddenly Joshua found himself wondering if Zoe had taken Samantha upstairs for a reason. Then he reached into his sweatshirt pocket. "I found something after you guys ran out in the snow. It must've fallen out of her suitcase."

"Just please tell me it's not another explosive device or warning from Magpie—"

Alex reached into his pocket. "Not quite."

A flash of light filled Joshua's eyes. He blinked. The most dazzling piece of jewelry he'd ever seen sparkled in Alex's hand.

"What am I looking at?"

Alex held up the string of diamonds and rubies like he was holding a tiny garter snake by the tail. "If it's real, I'm guessing about ten thousand dollars' worth of jewelry."

TWELVE

Samantha pushed the bathroom door open, sending a gust of steam billowing out into the upstairs hallway. When she'd come upstairs, she'd discovered Zoe had already gone ahead and pulled a warm gray sweatshirt and yoga pants from her suitcase for her to change into before running the water. Now Zoe was perched on a chair in the hallway, her slender, muscular legs folded under her like a teenager. Joshua had told her that Zoe had been hired as a bodyguard for Daniel's new private security business, and certainly, she'd seemed unflappable in a crisis.

Zoe looked up with a smile that was both trustworthy and disarming without being either cutesy or soft. Yes, Samantha had no doubt that in the right moment, Zoe was exactly the kind of person someone could trust their life to.

"Feeling better?" Zoe asked.

"Yes, much. Thank you." Hot water and a change of warm clean clothes had made all the difference to her body. But had done little to calm the turmoil in her heart from the unexpected kiss in the kitchen. "What time is it anyway?"

"Just past five in the morning," Zoe said. She yawned. "I don't know about you, but I'm probably going to head back to sleep for another hour or two."

"I'm sorry, I woke you."

"It's okay." Zoe unfolded and stood. "These things happen. We all have our issues and can't always control when or how they pop up."

"Well, I really appreciate it." Samantha slung the towel around her shoulders and turned off the bathroom light. "Most people wouldn't be this cool about someone waking everyone else up by screaming in the middle of the night and running around in the darkness."

She meant it as a bit of a joke, poking fun at herself to lighten the mood.

But Zoe didn't smile. "Joshua, Alex and I aren't most people."

There was an edge to her voice, a warning even, that Samantha couldn't quite translate.

"Well, thanks again for all your help. I hope

you manage to get some sleep." Samantha turned and started for the stairs.

Zoe touched her elbow.

"Look, it's not my place to say anything," she said. "But Joshua is a good guy. A really good guy. One of the best I know. Honest. Honorable. Steady. Like a second big brother to me."

Samantha turned back. "Joshua seems really fantastic."

She could still feel the pressure of Zoe's fingertips on her skin.

"Then don't hurt him," Zoe said plainly. "Be really clear and really direct about who you are and what you want right now. Look, I don't know what your deal is or what you're going through, and I'm not going to judge you. But I've seen the way he looks at you. He's got some pretty strong feelings for you already. He grew up without a single reliable woman in his life, and you two barely know each other. You could hurt him pretty badly, whether you mean to or not."

"Okay. I hear you. Thank you." It seemed the safest thing to say and once again totally inadequate for the conflicting thoughts and feelings cascading through her heart and mind.

Samantha went downstairs to the kitchen.

The clock over the stove was ending closer toward five thirty. Four and a half hours until her appointment with Theresa. Five and a half until she headed for the train station. Six until she was gone from Joshua's life. And he was gone from hers. Joshua and Alex were sitting in the living room, on opposite sides of the coffee table, their head bowed together over Alex's laptop computer. Her tablet was propped up beside it. But whatever they were looking at, they leaped up the moment she walked in.

"Hey." Her voice felt weak between her lips, as if it still wasn't sure it was ready to return.

Joshua stood, his eyes on her face and his back to the dark sky filling the windows behind him. A fresh khaki sweatshirt hung open over a plain white T-shirt. Blue jeans hung loose from his hips. Her heart flipped a beat. He was the most handsome man she'd ever seen. The bravest. The strongest. The kindest. It was like since she'd met him something had started filling up inside her, slowly and steadily, until it was ready to burst her heart open from the inside.

All this time, she'd thought she was incapable of ever feeling drawn to anyone. Like the night back in the dorm room had broken her heart's ability to beat. Now here was the wrong man, in the wrong place, at the wrong time. But somehow he was unlocking her heart in ways she didn't even think were possible.

And here she was staring at him, not knowing what to say to him. While his hazel eyes scanned her face, like he didn't know what to say to her either.

Alex crossed the room toward her. "Feeling better?"

It was the same question his sister had asked, in the same tone of voice.

"Yes. Much. Thank you. I'm so sorry I woke you guys up. Your sister's gone back to bed."

"No worries." Alex glanced from her to Joshua. "I'm going to go and try to get some more sleep too. If you need me, you know where to find me."

Alex closed the living room door behind him. Samantha sat down on a chair. Joshua sat down opposite her. Her lips still felt the faint tingle of his mouth on hers. Did he regret the spur-of-the-moment kiss? Had the overwhelming relief of being alive just gotten the better of them? Or did it mean as much to him as it did to her? She didn't know how to find the words for what she was thinking and feeling.

And for a long moment, neither of them said anything.

"How does your story end?" Joshua asked. Something soft moved through the strength in his voice. "The one you were telling me out in the snow."

"I don't really know if it has an end," she said. "That's the worst thing about it. I don't know why that guy broke into my room that night and attacked me. I went to the campus police the next morning, and they fired all sorts of questions at me, and I didn't know how to even answer them. Was it possible I'd let him in? Was it possible my door was open? Could I have invited him in? Had I ever led him to believe I was romantically interested in him? Could I have imagined the whole thing because I'd taken half a sleeping pill? Was it possible I'd dreamed it? They told me I couldn't file an official police report without any 'real' information. It wasn't until years later, when I was working at *Torchlight* that I learned that actually I could've. Since police use multiple reports to build crime maps, even when they don't have enough information to arrest someone with a crime, they still find the information useful, even if it has gaps and is incomplete." She leaned her head into her hands and looked down at her knees. "Anyway, that's really all there is to the story. I barely knew him. One night he attacked me. I fought him and ran, before he could do any real damage. I didn't even have bruises the next day. He was suspended, I think, and made to move buildings. I never really saw him again, just a couple of glimpses in crowded places where I wasn't even sure it was him."

She looked up at him. "Campus security told me if I couldn't remember then it probably didn't really happen. But I felt different. I felt like something was wrong with me, something was broken in me. Then the nightmares started. Like I was reliving it in my sleep but couldn't remember it when I woke up. I saw a counselor on campus at the time and he told me the night terrors would go away when I made peace with what had happened. But how do you make peace with something that you don't remember? I never went to the police beyond the ones on campus that pooh-poohed me. I never charged him with a crime. I can't do anything about it now."

"I'm sorry," Joshua said.

"The worst thing is the feeling that I'm

never going to understand it. Because there's no way to understand it. And if I can't understand it, I can't fix my memory of it."

"I know the feeling." A sad chuckle crossed his lips. "Few years back, I was driving with some friends in a jeep convoy through a territory that was supposed to be safe and suddenly this blast hits the jeep in front of us. Comes out of nowhere. But just like that one guy's dead and two more have serious injuries. And you know what the worst part was? For months afterwards every single time somebody in that region gave us the stink-eye—even hours away from that place, all I could think was, 'Was it you? Was it you who did that?' Because, somehow, part of me just couldn't let go of the need to know who that person was who hurt and killed my friends, so I could make sure he faced justice. Nobody likes to think life's a series of bad, random things that happen for no reason. So, we all try to put our own sense to it."

"Because if you can make everything fit together, it's logical and you can fix it," she said. "And you can stop it from happening again."

"Yeah." He nodded. "My grandfather served in the military. In a way Gramps was a series of contradictions, because he never stopped

trying to rationalize exactly why my grandmother died and why my mother left, so I
could learn from his mistakes and wouldn't
ever go through either of those types of pains.
But one of the wisest things he used to say
was that life was like a jigsaw puzzle you find
in the bottom of the closet. If we're blessed,
we'll be able to put enough of it together to
get a bigger picture to go by. But sometimes,
our puzzle's going to be missing a few pieces.
Sometimes our puzzles are going to have spare
pieces in them that actually belong to other
puzzles, and if we're not careful we'll drive
ourselves crazy trying to make them fit somewhere they don't belong."

"Yeah," she said. She'd gotten into her job
because she liked knowing that sometimes
it was possible to collect even the hardest-
to-find pieces and put impossible puzzles
together. "I just don't want this thing with
Magpie to be yet another thing that I have to
accept will never make sense."

"I know," he said, "and I've been praying
that it won't be."

She looked down at the tiny sliver of space
between his body and hers. His hands rested
on his knees, just a tiny motion away from her
fingers. Something inside her ached to feel
the comforting strength of his arms around

her again, to run her hands around his neck and pull him close and feel his warm lips brush against hers again.

You're going to hurt him, if you're not careful. Zoe's voice echoed in her ears. He deserved better than a dented, battered heart like hers, that wasn't even sure it knew how to beat.

The fire crackled gently in the fireplace. The snow lightened its steady beat against the window.

"Anyway," she said. "You said we need to talk."

"We do." Joshua shifted in his seat. "Alex found this on the floor."

He reached down beside him on the chair and pulled out a string of diamonds and rubies in a vintage setting. It flashed in the firelight, and it took her a moment to even realize it was the same jewelry she'd gotten from Eric.

"That's what was in the gift that Eric left on my door." She stretched out her hand. "It's his Christmas present to me. I'm going to talk to him about it after the holidays."

He didn't hand it to her. "But I thought you'd told me you'd made it clear you didn't want to be in a romantic relationship with him?"

"I have." A flush rose to her cheeks. Had

he seen and read the note? Giving a trinket to a girl was a bit pushy, but hardly a crime. "Maybe he's just way too generous with his friends. Either way I'm going to have to talk to him again and make it clearer."

He hesitated another moment and then handed her the bracelet. She stuffed it into her pocket.

"Are you sure you should be going around with something like this in your pocket? It could make you a target. I never even considered that money could be a factor in any of what you're going through. If he's given you multiple pieces like this, and people know that you're carrying them, it could be a serious motive. People have killed for less."

"Less than what? He told me it was just some old piece of jewelry his mom thought I'd like. Or something like that. Although, considering the lie he told you about the nature of our relationship, it might be even more likely he went overboard, splashed out a couple hundred for it, and then made up some story about some mother I've never met because he thought that sounded better."

"It's worth almost ten thousand dollars."

"What?" She yanked it out of her pocket and dropped it on the coffee table like some kind of deadly thorn. It lay there and glittered at her in the firelight. "You can't be serious."

Yes, he was a popular radio host. But that didn't mean he'd splash out that much money on his friends, even friends he had a crush on.

"Alex's mother—Zoe's stepmother—is a very wealthy woman. He recognized the designer's stamp and looked it up online. It's not actually old, it was just designed to look old. Comparable items sell anywhere from seven to ten thousand." He turned the laptop around. It was open to a jewelry website. "If someone knew you had a wealthy romantic suitor, even if you weren't accepting their advances, that would give them a reason to go after you. This could be that missing piece you were talking about. That one fact to pull everything together and make sense of everything."

"Or it could be one of those random, spare pieces from that puzzle metaphor that belong to a completely different puzzle! This bracelet might not even be real. It could just be some knockoff he picked up somewhere for next to nothing. He knows I like secondhand stores. They sell a lot of fake jewelry." True, fake jewelry didn't usually glisten and glitter like that. She picked up her tablet, zoomed in, and took a picture of the jewelry. "Or he could've picked it up from a secondhand shop that didn't know what it was worth. I'll email the designer and see if they can tell me more about it. I'm sure they'd be happy to authenticate it for me."

"So you agree that Eric could have something to do with what's happened to you?"

"Maybe. I don't know. He certainly still seems hung up on my neighbor, which is how I met him in the first place." She stood. He stood too. Why was he pushing this? "Yes, Eric might have a crush on me. And sure, he doesn't like the fact I'm a workaholic who doesn't have time for coffee and apparently isn't ready to be in a romantic relationship with anyone." No matter how hard her heart beat whenever Joshua was around. "But he had no motive for hiring someone to kidnap me, dump me in the middle of nowhere and threaten my life. He's not vicious. He's very, very protective of me. He's like a big sad but also hyper puppy dog who's been dumped too many times."

Joshua crossed his arms. "Even sad puppy dogs bite."

"Yes. Fine. Sometimes they do. And like I said, I'll email the company right away and see what they can tell me about the piece. I promise I won't be alone with Eric, if that makes you feel better. Eric's behavior has been iffy recently. Even for him. Maybe he's increased the dosage on the amount of caffeine he's using to get buzzed in the morning. I thought he was over Bella, or had at least made peace with her leaving. But then today he was all worried that something bad might have happened to her. I told him about Roy and that seemed to set him off. But I'll return the jewelry and I'll tell the police about it."

Why had he turned this into an argument? And why was he pushing so hard on the topic of Eric? It was like a wedge to push her away.

Here they were, alone together, in the darkened living room, standing face-to-face, so close she could almost feel the heat of his breath. He'd risked his life to save her. He'd carried her in his arms through a snowstorm. She'd shared with him the darkest secret in her heart, right here in this firelight. They'd shared an all-too-brief but affectionate kiss. Yet, rather than hugging and reassuring her as a friend would, he was quizzing her about her relationship with Eric. He'd even searched out her bracelet online while she was upstairs.

She stepped toward him. Her earnest gaze met his. "I thought we were on the same team. Why does it feel like you're investigating me?"

"I'm trying to protect you." Joshua sighed like a man twenty years older than he was. "I'm trying to keep you alive. And to do that I can't be your buddy, or best friend or…" He stepped back and ran both hands through his hair. "And I can't be holding you in my arms or kissing you like I did. I'm sorry. That was out of line, and I apologize. Protecting you is the most important thing. And I think it's time I took a step back and started acting like a bodyguard."

The click-clack of Samantha typing on the tablet filtered through the closed study door. Joshua stretched out on the couch again. But he didn't sleep.

Instead he lay there, staring at the ceiling and wanting things he didn't know how to put into words. How was it even possible to feel like this about someone? To feel so drawn to them? To feel like…like there'd been a part of himself missing all this time and he'd found it in someone else's eyes. Like she was a part of him he didn't want to live without. He groaned and punched the pillow behind his head until it fit more comfortably under his neck.

I married your mother because I was lonely, Dad had told him one day when they were working side by side in the workshop, after fleeing another one of Gramps's epic rants. *It was love at first sight. I was eating with my friends in a pizza joint. She walked in the door. And bam. I fell boots over brains for her. I asked her to marry me too soon. She said yes too soon. We were young and dumb. She wasn't happy. I asked her to stay. She didn't.*

He stood up and started pacing and praying. His eyes darted from the darkness outside to her closed door to the minutes ticking past on the clock.

He wasn't sure exactly what he felt for Samantha. But he did want what was best for her. She deserved a hero. She deserved someone who was going to stick around and be there for her.

She deserved a man better than Joshua Rhodes.

He sighed. Was that it? Samantha deserved so many good things in life and a man who could give them to her. Not a man at a crossroads who had no way of knowing where his life was heading or even if he still wanted to stay in the career he'd committed his life to.

Alex came downstairs an hour later, put on a pot of coffee and then went outside to shovel out his truck. Joshua followed. Slowly, as the day rose around them, Joshua and Alex stood in the winter cold and methodically dug out the driveway.

"Daniel needs a snowblower," Alex said. He leaned his shoulder into the shovel and drove it through the snow. "Who in their right mind owns a property this big without one?"

"He probably has one, and we haven't found it yet." Joshua chuckled. His eyes rose to where the crisp morning sun was rising in a crystal-clear blue sky, sending light dazzling over last night's deep snow. He could still see just the very faintest of imprints in the snow from where he and Samantha had trudged the night before. A shiver ran down his spine. They really could've frozen to death just twenty steps from safety.

"I should come with you," Alex said. "I don't like the idea of you two going alone."

"What, are you worried I'll crash your truck like you crashed mine?" Joshua asked.

Alex didn't laugh at the joke.

"Don't worry," Joshua said. "We'll be fine. All I need to do is drive Samantha to Theresa's office. I'll wait outside, guarding the door pretty much while they talk. Then I'll drive her to the train station and wait while she sorts out her train. I'll be back here in time for dinner. Simple, really."

So simple somehow it felt wrong. Like it shouldn't be this easy for them to just walk out of each other's lives this way.

"I know," Alex said. He yanked off his hat and ran his hand through his hair. "I just hate the idea of my personal stuff getting in the way of my being there for you."

He meant Theresa.

"We both know that if I asked you to come, you would," Joshua said. "But I honestly don't think you need to. I'm sure we'll be okay."

Alex nodded. A frown crossed his face, like he was looking at something a very long way away.

"How long has it been since you last saw Theresa?" Joshua asked.

"We've nodded and made meaningless chitchat a few times in passing when we happened to be at the same event. But we haven't actually had a real conversation about anything since the day she handed me back the ring and ended our engagement. Zoe still can't even look her in the eye."

Joshua nodded slowly. Yeah, he'd figured as much. Not that Alex had ever said much about it. For all his casual small talk, Alex was as unforthcoming about emotional things as Dad was.

"You never told me what happened there,"

Joshua admitted. "Not why you decided to marry her. Not why you decided to call the wedding off. None of it."

"I wanted to marry Theresa Vaughan," Alex said. "Very much, in fact. She made me feel like the best version of myself. It was like simply being around her made me feel like a better man, while simultaneously making me want to keep striving to be an even better man than I was." He looked back down at Joshua. "She decided she didn't want to marry me because she didn't think I had what it took to be the kind of husband she needed me to be. I couldn't settle in a job. I couldn't commit to a career. Our lives were heading in very different directions."

A door clattered behind them. He turned back. Samantha leaned out the doorway and held up two mugs of coffee. He nodded. She slipped back inside.

"I know the feeling."

"Are you sure?" Alex dropped his shovel in the snow. "Because looks more to me like you're standing at a crossroads, waiting for someone to come along and push you into making a decision. You think Daniel, Zoe and I wouldn't ask you in a heartbeat to leave the military and come work with us? We need your skills, mate. None of us think the way

you do. Our team's not complete without you.
But I know you, Josh. I know you only joined
the army because your gramps pushed you to.
And that your dad pushed you just as hard to
become a cop. So, there's no way I'm going to
push you into being anything, or doing anything, you don't choose. Now, I'm not claiming to understand what's going on between
you and Samantha. But there's something
there. As far as I can see, she's not the kind
to person to push you into something either.
So if you don't know how she fits in your life,
then maybe it's because you still haven't decided what you want your life to be. Maybe
she's nothing more than a reminder that you
need to." He turned and started for the door.
"And I'm getting coffee."

Zoe didn't come down for breakfast and it
seemed Samantha didn't feel much like talking. So breakfast was quick and quiet. They
set off on the drive back to Toronto. Bright
sunlight filtered through the windshield. Endless dazzling white spread out in all directions. Samantha's eyes were locked on the
world outside her window. But not like she
was upset. More like she was deep in thought.
Or even praying.

Theresa lived on the very northerly outskirts of Toronto, in a small town that had just recently been swept up in the growth of the city moving north. He drove down a beautifully maintained old-fashioned main street. The street was deserted. Lights were off. Stores were closed. Yet, a bright light shone over the door leading to Palm Branches Counseling. He pulled into the small parking lot and turned off the engine. Then he reached over and squeezed her hand.

"Don't worry," he said. "Theresa is amazing. You two are going to get along great."

Samantha squeezed him back. A smile flashed in her eyes. Then she reached around his neck and gave him a hug so quick he barely had time to raise his arms and hug her back before she pulled away.

"Thank you for everything," she said. "I'm sorry I don't say this more, but you've really been wonderful and I'm so grateful."

I'm not claiming to understand what's going on between you and Samantha. Alex's words echoed in his mind. *But there's something there. As far as I can see, she's not the kind of person to push you into something either.*

He felt her fingers brush against his hands. He looked down. She'd slid the bracelet into his hand.

"Take care of this for me, please," she said. "I'd feel more comfortable knowing you were holding on to it. Not that I'm ready to believe it's worth all the money you say it's worth. I still haven't heard back from the company so I'm still hoping it's just a cheap knockoff. I can't imagine Eric or anyone spending that much money on me." She hugged him again, and for a moment he felt his skin shiver as her lips brushed over his cheek. Then she shoved the truck door open.

"You're more than worth it," Joshua blurted.

She froze, her hand on the open door. A question hovered in her eyes.

"The bracelet, I mean," he said. "Whether it's worth a hundred dollars or a hundred thousand, doesn't change the fact that you're the kind of person who's worth giving something that valuable to. Giving everything valuable to."

A flush rose to her cheeks. She opened her mouth but no words came out. The front door of Palm Branches opened and Theresa stood there in the doorway, her long dark hair held back in a braid. Samantha turned and walked toward her.

"Thanks again for the ride," Samantha called back to him over her shoulder. "I've got your number in my phone. I'll call you when we're done."

The women talked for a minute, and then Samantha disappeared inside.

Theresa smiled and waved at the truck.

He rolled down the window and leaned out. "Hey! Theresa!"

"Joshua! Hi! You're welcome to come in and sit in the waiting room. Or there's a really good café just a couple of doors down. Might be open already."

"Thank you." He nodded. "I might take you up on that. But first I think I'm going to stretch my legs a bit and take a look around. Remind Samantha that she has my number in her phone if she needs me."

His legs felt jittery. His skin felt like it was on fire. What had he been thinking, just blurting something out like that?

"Okay," Theresa called. "Will do. We should be about an hour. The front door is locked. So when you come back, ring the bell and I'll open the door for you."

She popped back inside. He heard the door lock behind her.

He squared his shoulders. Right. So he had an hour to think about the fact he'd just told a woman who was about to leave his life in a couple of hours that he thought she was worth a king's ransom. And figure out what to do about it.

He started walking along the narrow main street. A park lay at one end. More shops at the other. He chose north toward the shops. His eyes scanned the empty boutique stores on both sides. Should he look for a Christmas present for her? Something cute? Something small and thoughtful? What do you give a beautiful woman who's already been given thousands of dollars in jewels? Something equally extraordinary for an extraordinary woman?

A young man emerged from a side alley and started walking down the empty street toward him. His head was buried deep inside the hood of his sweatshirt. His hands were buried in his pockets. The right one bulged. A knife? A weapon? A wallet? A phone? Funny, how much bodyguard mode felt so very much like soldier mode. Maybe Alex was right. Maybe he had been pushed into a military career. Maybe Gramps had pushed him in one direction and Dad had pushed him into another.

If we don't push you, you'll end trying to start some crazy business with your foolish buddy Alex! Gramps would say, back when it looked like Alex was going to drift aimlessly through life forever. *Is that what you really want?*

It hadn't been. Not back then. He'd honestly wanted to tackle a real career, learning exactly the kind of military skills he'd used in the last few days to become the man he was and to keep Samantha safe. But Gramps had always underestimated Alex.

Might've even underestimated Joshua too.

The youth grew closer, with that purposeful arrogant walk that said he wasn't about to give up an inch of snowy sidewalk that he didn't have to. Joshua laughed under his breath and stepped aside to let him past. But with a sudden, aggressive move, the youth bodychecked Joshua so hard it would've sent a weaker man sprawling onto the ice.

The youth snickered. The hood fell back.

His eyes met Joshua's.

Joshua stared. No, it couldn't be.

It was Hermes!

The graffiti artist who'd broken into the *Torchlight News* office yesterday, scrawled a message from Magpie on the wall and threatened Samantha. And here he was, almost an hour's drive north, on a snowy, deserted street, in a completely different part of the city. It didn't make sense. There was no logical reason for him to be there. It was yet another piece that didn't come close to fitting into anything Joshua thought he knew about the puzzle.

Yet here Hermes was. Staring him down. Like a challenge. Like he was daring Joshua to do something about it. This time, there was no way Joshua was about to let him get away. For a long moment, Hermes stood there on the cold, icy street, staring at Joshua with a hard, empty look. Then he spat on the ground at Joshua's feet and swore. "You got me arrested."

"You got yourself arrested. And you should still be in jail."

"Magpie bailed me out." An ugly smile spread across Hermes's face. "Magpie has my back."

Joshua's eyes scanned the empty streets. "Who's Magpie?"

Hermes laughed. "Wouldn't you like to know?"

"Is it a person? Is it a group? Is he why you're here? Did he send you here?"

Hermes laughed. Then he crossed his arms. "A hundred thou."

Joshua blinked. "Excuse me?"

The graffiti artist talked slowly, with a lilting, singsong swagger.

"You give me one hundred thousand dollars, and I'll tell you who Magpie is, what Magpie really wants and what Magpie's going to do to that pretty little girlfriend of yours. It's up to you and how much you value your girlie's life. Or she'll be dead by Christmas."

THIRTEEN

Joshua reached in his pocket and yanked out the phone. "How about you tell it to the police?"

Hermes slugged him in the jaw. Joshua blocked the blow, but not before his phone slipped from his hand and hit the ice. Hermes spun on his heels and took off running down the street.

Joshua groaned, snatched up his phone and ran after him.

Why does anybody in this day and age need a bodyguard? Isn't that what the police are for? The arrogant way he'd challenged Daniel when he'd first heard about Ash Private Security now clattered in his mind. No wonder Daniel hadn't offered him a job. Joshua had been too busy repeating the same claptrap he'd heard from his grandfather a hundred times before.

The police couldn't always protect people like Samantha. But he could.

Hermes raced down the main street, slipped into a side alley and cut behind a building. Joshua followed. But the kid was fast, pelting through the icy, urban obstacles like he knew exactly where he was going. Hermes scaled a fence, sprinted across the road and ran hard for the park. Yellow and orange barricades crossed the entrance warning the paths and bridge were closed and dangerous because of the ice. Hermes leaped the barrier. He tumbled into the snow, scrambled back to his feet and kept running toward the trees. Joshua followed, gaining ground with every step until the youth was only a few paces ahead. The path was slick and covered in snow. Snow twinkled from the bare branches.

A frozen river lay to his right, gray water rippling between gaps in sheets of ice. Hermes sprinted onto the narrow wooden bridge that spanned it. His feet slipped. Joshua leaped, caught Hermes by the legs and brought him down. Their bodies hit the icy wood. Hermes flailed and tried to struggle to his feet. Joshua's hands struggled to pin him, reaching for the bulge of a gun he'd seen in Hermes's pocket. What was Hermes thinking? Joshua would beat him again, like he'd beaten him before.

Then he smelled a stench of old tobacco. A second young man, with a nasty scar spanning his face, stepped out from behind the bushes on one side of the bridge. Then a third in a ratty jacket and a sneer of missing teeth, appeared on the other side of the bridge.

The men who'd kidnapped and terrorized Samantha. They'd lured him to the bridge and trapped him there.

"Let Hermes go! Now!" the one who smelled of cigarettes shouted. His voice was filled with rage and reeked with the desire to hurt someone.

Joshua stood up slowly, letting Hermes scramble away from him to join the others. "I don't need to fight you. We can talk this out. Tell me who you are and what Magpie wants with Samantha Colt."

The one with missing teeth laughed—a cold, nasty sound like a wild animal wheezing. Then they charged. The one with missing teeth got to Joshua first. A hammer was clenched in his grasp. Joshua met him head-on, leveling a blow to his chest and knocking the weapon from his hands. Then the one who reeked of cigarettes jumped on him from behind, and it was two against one, leaving

Joshua with nothing but his strength and his wits, as he blocked, weaved and defended against the onslaught. A knife flashed before his eyes. With a swift twist of his wrist, he wrenched it from the smoker's hand, even as he felt his accomplice's fist crack hard against his skull. Pain ricocheted through his body. The crack of a gun split the winter air. And that was when he realized they wanted him dead. They'd lured him out here to kill him, in this isolated, cold, icy, snowy park where he'd fall unconscious in the snow before anybody found his body.

God, please, forgive me. I should never have let myself be lured away from Samantha.

He had to get back to her. He had to protect her. Nothing else mattered.

"Get him and force him down." Hermes walked toward him. A gun shook in his hands. He aimed at Joshua's head and something told the soldier that this time Hermes's weapon wasn't loaded with blanks. "Magpie says we've just got to kill him. Whatever it takes. We just got to get it done. Then we're done. We don't got to kill or kidnap anybody else."

"Done what?" Joshua called. "Listen to me, whatever Magpie is they can't make you do anything."

The bad-smelling youth tried to grab onto his arms now. He tossed him off, just as the second one dove for his legs. Joshua slid on the ice and barely caught himself from falling. He couldn't keep fighting, trapped on the bridge, three against one. His only hope was to bulldoze his way through them, leap to shore and run, hoping Hermes wouldn't be able to make the shot.

A second bullet flew from Hermes's gun, tearing off a chunk of the railing.

"Watch it!" The thug who was missing teeth swore.

"Then grab him and hold him still!"

One way or the other, he had to get off this bridge. The thugs lunged at him again. Joshua tossed them off and ran. But slick ice beneath tore his footing out from under him. He hit the bridge and rolled off. He fell. He felt his body break through the ice. Freezing cold water rushed over his head.

A flurry of bullets filled the air as Hermes stood over him and fired.

It was a calm space, Samantha thought. Everything about Palm Branches was soothing, from the green walls to the trickle of water cascading from the marble rock fountain on a table to her left. A beautiful towering ficus rose like a tree in a terra-cotta pot by the door. She didn't know what she'd expected the room to be like. A medical center maybe? A doctor's office? Instead, this was like visiting the very cool, very chic home of an awesome friend who was willing to listen and didn't mind if you started stories in the wrong place or told them in the wrong order.

"The scariest thing about what happened in college is the way the nightmares keep coming back every now and then," Samantha said. "I might go months, even years, without one. Then suddenly I'll be researching something that reminds me of that night and they start up again. Now I'm worried the same thing's going to happen about this. I want closure, I just don't know how to get it."

"Maybe it would help you to put some of this down on paper," Theresa said. She poured the last of the jasmine tea into their two cups. "You never know, it could help readers who've gone through similar trauma. Even if you say you're just a fact-checker, you've got a story in you—a story you might feel better if you told. I think you were very brave—both in what happened to you in college and what happened yesterday. You're a fighter. In a way you've never stopped fighting what happened. Maybe you need to find a new way to fight. Or a way to accept you've done all you can do."

Samantha drained her cup. "Joshua keeps comparing me to a soldier."

"Is that helpful?" Theresa set her teapot down.

"Yeah, he's a good listener. He makes me feel like I'm less broken inside than I thought I was." She drained her cup and set it down. "I've never met anyone like him."

Theresa's eyes rose to the wall and only then did Samantha realize they'd been talking for over an hour. Joshua must be bored stiff waiting for them.

"Can I ask you a question?" Samantha asked.

"Sure."

"You known Joshua a long time," she said. "Why do you think he's still single?"

"You'd have to ask Joshua that." Theresa stood and picked up the tea tray. "But I will say that the Joshua I've always known is a protector. It really matters to him that he can take care of those in his life that he cares about. As you know, he was raised by two men who held him to very high standards. He holds himself to those standards too. I'm just going to pop out and tell him that we'll be another ten minutes or so."

Theresa slipped into the other room. Samantha pulled out her tablet. There was a new email message. She hadn't heard it come in. It was from the jewelry company.

Dear Ms. Colt,
Thank you for bringing the bracelet to our attention. It is indeed one of ours. It belonged to a Ms. Isobel Joy Niar, who gave us permission to contact anyone who came into contact with it. We are sure her next of kin will be happy to hear it has been retrieved…

Her heart stopped. Isobel *Joy Niar*? As in Isobel *Joyner*? The fourth woman on Roy Davis's list? Here she'd spent hours trying to track down any trace of the woman—not even realizing for a moment she might've gotten her name wrong. A chill ran down Samantha's spine. Had Eric bought her a dead woman's bracelet?

The front-door chimes sounded. She tapped the new name into the internet and the result she was looking for popped up instantly: Woman found dead in storage unit identified as model Isobel Joy Niar.

The article was dated two days ago. A picture loaded. It was Bella. She reached for her phone and dialed Joshua's number.

A scream came from the other room, filling the air for a fraction of a second before it was cut short. The front door slammed shut. She heard the lock click into place, then the muffled sound of Theresa whimpering and furniture scraping across the floor.

Slowly, Samantha rose slowly from her seat, like someone who was caught in a nightmare and couldn't wake up. Her heart pounded furiously in her throat.

Help me, Lord. Help me know what to do.

The phone was ringing but Joshua wasn't answering. She crept toward the flimsy glass door. Then through the crack she could see them. Theresa was standing, frozen. One hand clenched Theresa's throat. Another hand pressed a gun to her temple.

"Hey, Samantha?" a voice called. "You in here?"

The phone stopped ringing. She hit Redial. Then she took another step forward until she could see the clear, unmasked face of the man holding the gun to Theresa's face. *It was Eric.*

"Hey, Samantha? Where are you? We really need to talk!"

The glass door swung open. Samantha shoved her phone into her pocket praying for Joshua to answer. Theresa's body pushed through, a gun to her temple, her eyes wide with fear. Samantha forced her gaze on the man holding the gun.

"Eric, what do you think you're doing?"

"Samantha!" Eric smiled. His face was flushed, with the confusion and panic that clashed with the very deadly weapon he now held against Theresa's head. "I'm so glad I found you. Look, you're not going to believe this, but something really bad's going on. You need to come with me. Now."

A fighter. Joshua said I'm a fighter. But I don't want to fight. I don't know how to fight. I want to run.

"We can talk about whatever you want, but first you have to let Theresa go."

"I can't do that." Eric's head shook. His grip tightened around Theresa's throat. "Somebody's trying to kill you and she might be part of it. They're called Magpie. I don't know who they are. But they killed Bella too. They run around killing all the women I care about."

"Bella's real name is Isobel Joy Niar, right?" she said softly, feeling the pieces of the puzzle slowly fit together in her brain. "You were right all along. She didn't move out. She died and her body was hidden with her belongings in a storage unit. Then you gave me her bracelet."

"I didn't know it was hers." His head was shaking. "Or maybe I did, and I forgot. I've started forgetting a lot of things. I didn't know about the storage locker and I don't know why she died, Samantha! I don't. One day she was in my life. The next she was gone. Like my friend Jessica at the gym and Monique, who I became friends with at the coffee shop."

"And Holly, the girl you asked out in high school."

Eric is the missing link. The one thing that ties them all together. Joshua told me, and I didn't see it. Because something about it just didn't fit.

"I want to listen." She took another step forward. Theresa's frightened eyes met hers. If she could just create a distraction, Theresa could escape. "Please, help me understand. You're the Magpie, aren't you? Did you become the Magpie to hurt the women who hurt you? To kill them because you were afraid of losing them?"

"I didn't kill them!" His voice rose. "Somebody else did. I love them and they all died." A pitiful pleading filled his voice. "So I hired a private detective…"

"You hired Roy Davis?"

He nodded. "Yes! That's him. I found Roy online and explained to Roy that all these women had disappeared or died, and I thought someone had killed them, and that I'd pay him a lot of money to find out who. He asked if I knew who might die next, and I said maybe you."

Then Roy had gone snooping around the building, and her work, before somehow fixating on Joshua as a culprit. "Where's Roy now, Eric?"

"I don't know," Eric wailed. "He called me from jail and said he'd been arrested, but that he'd overheard someone talking about you coming here. Roy was the one who told me about Magpie. I hadn't even heard of Magpie until he told me. But now it all makes sense."

Did it? She prayed. *Help me God, what am I still not seeing?*

"So you're going to run away with me." Eric's bright blue eyes locked on her face. "Right now, today. Before Magpie can hurt you too. We'll get in my car, and drive and drive somewhere, until we're alone, somewhere nobody will ever find us. Okay. We'll be together, and love each other. I will protect you, and nobody will hurt you like the others."

God, please help me to be strong.

"No, Eric." She gritted her teeth and felt fresh strength move through her. "I will leave with you, if you promise not to hurt Theresa and let her go. But I will never love you."

Something dark glimmered in the cold blue of his eyes. He leaned in until she could almost feel his breath on her face. "Then you're going to die just like the rest of them."

FOURTEEN

Dark icy-cold water swirled beneath him. Freezing wood pressed against his back. Joshua gritted his teeth. They were chattering so badly he was afraid the group on the bridge could hear them. When his body had hit the water, he'd gone under, as an explosion of bullets had rained down around him, shattering the ice. He'd stayed under, fighting the current, as long as he dared, then when his lungs couldn't take any more punishment he'd swum underneath the bridge. Once there, he wedged himself in underneath the frozen wood, with the water flowing beneath him and his hands gripping the wood.

Rolling off the bridge seemed a better idea than staying up there, but still he was far from safe. He could hear them pacing above him, like sentries, or some weird reversal of a fairy tale about the troll who lived under a bridge. If he climbed up, Hermes would see him and shoot. If he tried to swim downstream and come up there, he'd freeze and drown in the icy depths of the river. And if he stayed there, wedged under the bridge, he'd be good for nothing. And he'd eventually fall.

"You see him?" Hermes asked.

"No," replied the one with missing teeth.

"Is he dead? He'd better be dead!"

"How am I supposed to know if he's dead?"

"Magpie wants him dead!"

"If you see him, shoot him."

"What about the girlie? Samantha?"

"Magpie said somebody else gets to have at her."

A brutal killer was going to get Samantha on behalf of the criminal mastermind behind all this, and all he could do was stay braced beneath a bridge, gasping for breath, feeling the growing weakness in his limbs threatening to send him tumbling back into the water.

Moments ago, his phone had started ringing, clattering above him on the bridge from where it must've fallen in the fight. Seconds later it was flung off the bridge, and he watched, helpless, as it skittered across the ice. His heart lurched as he saw the name on the screen before it slipped into a crack and disappeared beneath the ice. *Samantha.* Samantha was alive and calling him for help. And he couldn't save her.

God, my gramps taught me that no matter how lost and wrong someone gets, they can always turn to You and that You will guide their steps. I don't know if Alex is right, and that I let myself get pushed into the life I'm living now, out of a sense of duty, rather than charting my own path. But I need Your help right now. Help me know what choices to make and what actions to take. And more than anything please help me know how to help Samantha. Don't let her get hurt because of me.

He heard a woman giggling in the distance. The sound was so unusual and unexpected, he didn't know what to make of it. It was bitterly cold and the park was closed. Who in their right mind would go out for a winter's stroll on a day like this? Straining his neck, he looked down the path. There were two figures, heavily wrapped up against the cold, wandering through the park toward the bridge. Joshua gave a quick thanks to God. It might not be the distraction he would have chosen. But he would take it and be grateful.

Slowly, he unwound his body. Slipping sideways, he braced his legs against the support beams and climbed his way under to the far side of the bridge.

"Hey! Stop!" Hermes shouted. "You two! Go back. This bridge is closed."

The couple kept walking, like they didn't hear him. The two other young men walked down to the foot of the bridge toward the couple.

"Stop! Stop now!" Hermes sounded panicked, almost hysterical.

Joshua braced his full weight into his arms, gripped the far side of the bridge and pulled himself up, enough that he could look over the edge.

Hermes had run to the far side of the bridge. He waved his gun hysterically at the approaching couple. "Turn around and leave!"

Hermes raised his gun to fire what Joshua hoped was supposed to be a warning shot. Not that he was about to get the opportunity. Joshua hauled himself up onto the bridge, launching himself on his stomach. He grabbed Hermes by the ankles. The gun went off. The bullet flew high into the air. Hermes fell forward onto the bridge. Joshua dragged himself up onto the bridge without letting go.

The couple were now running through the snow toward the bridge. Joy exploded in Joshua's heart. It was Alex and Zoe. The one with missing teeth charged at them. Alex launched himself headfirst at him in the football tackle, crashing into him and bringing him down into the snow. The one who stank of cigarettes turned tail and ran.

"Josh? You okay?" Zoe was running toward them.

I am now.

Hermes was still thrashing like a wild animal, trying to claw his way from Joshua's grasp. Zoe scooped his gun up from where it had landed. Her steady grip pointed it at Hermes. "Stop fighting my friend, or I'm shooting you in the leg. Trust me, I'm not going to miss."

Hermes fell still. Joshua wrenched his hands behind his back.

"What are you doing here?" Joshua asked.

Zoe grabbed a pair of zip ties out of her jacket pocket and made quick work tying Hermes's hands. "When I woke up and you were gone, my brother and I had words. I might not like what happened between Theresa and Alex. But you still shouldn't be heading into something like this without backup."

"I told him I didn't need backup."

"Well, you were wrong, weren't you?" A smile turned on her lips. She tossed Alex a second pair of zip ties. He caught them and handcuffed the other thug. "We took my car, since you'd taken the truck. We got to Theresa's and couldn't find you. But it was pretty clear from the footsteps in the snow that some kind of chase had happened. So we followed them to the park, and then we heard the gunshots."

Hopefully someone else would've heard them too, and called 911.

He leaped to his feet. "I've got to get back to Palm Branches. Killing me was a distraction. The real target they're after is Samantha. Call the police. Then call Daniel and fill him in. I'm going after Samantha and Theresa."

"You want us to come with you?" Zoe shouted after him.

"Yes, but it's more important these two don't get away again. So make sure you hold him until police get here, then make sure the police know they tried to kill us. Last thing we want is Hermes getting back out on the street again."

Joshua pelted through the snow, praying with every breath that he'd get to Theresa's offices and find Samantha there safe and sound. His senses strained for the sight and sound of police and emergency vehicles heading their way. But the street was just as empty as before. His feet pelted up the road.

His heart prayed. He reached the storefront and froze.

Now what? Do I knock? Do I presume she's in danger?

He looked down. Three sets of footsteps led in. No footsteps leading out.

There was somebody else in there.

He looked around at the empty sky.

God, I don't know if it's true that love makes a man stupid. Maybe it depends on the man. Maybe it depends on the type of love. I don't even know what to call what I'm feeling right now. But my heart tells me that Samantha's in trouble and that she needs me.

Carefully he tried the door. It was locked. He peered in the front window. The front room was empty, but through the frosted divider he could see three figures in the second room. A man standing with a gun in his hand. Two women sitting back to back. Joshua reached into his pocket. He had nothing. Not even his phone. All he had were the keys to Alex's truck.

A grim smile crossed his lips. He climbed inside and gunned the engine.

Samantha's hands were tied behind her back. The gag pressed tightly into her mouth. Behind her she could feel Theresa's hands against hers. Theresa wasn't moving. Her pulse was faint under Samantha's fingertips. *Just how hard had Eric struck her?* Tears filled Samantha's eyes. Desperate, wordless prayers filled her lungs. Worry for Joshua filled her heart. He should be here. If he wasn't here, something was very wrong.

Joshua wouldn't ever let her down.

Eric was standing in the doorway, leaning out through the glass doorway, looking into the main room, as if he was waiting for someone to arrive. Waiting for Magpie to show up and kill her?

"I'm sorry I knocked her out." He turned back. "But I didn't want her listening. I don't know if she was part of it or if we could trust her."

Part of the fact that women he was infatuated with kept disappearing and dying.

Then a thought hit her like a punch in the gut. Everything she'd found in ATHENA had assured her that Eric wasn't dangerous. But there were facts Samantha hadn't known, facts her database hadn't been able to find and put together.

She closed her eyes. Maybe it was impossible to know all the facts. Ever. People weren't like numbers on a sheet. Joshua's gut had told him Eric was part of what had happened to Samantha all along. But she just hadn't seen it.

Samantha squeezed Theresa's fingers.

Please Lord, get us out of here alive.

"Look at me!" Eric barked. She opened her eyes. The gun waved in her face. "Now, it's very important you understand that I didn't kill anyone. I really did go looking for you in the hospital. I wanted to see if Magpie had killed you. And I've known for a long time that whoever had made Holly disappear is who made Bella disappear too." *Did he not know that Holly had drowned? Had he really not known that Bella had turned up dead in a storage locker?* "I tried to warn you, though. I just had to be subtle about it, because I didn't know how far it had gone, or how much you knew. Because I knew by then, women I love disappear. Sure, when Holly disappeared in high school I didn't think much of it. But then Jessica died, and Monique, and then Bella disappeared, and I realized someone was disposing of women who weren't good enough for me. That's why I hired Roy to find this person, so I can explain to Magpie that I don't want them to kill you. I wanted them to give you an opportunity to show you really cared about me. Now Magpie's going to come and try to kill you, and I'll finally know who they are. Because Magpie's just trying to protect me. Just like I'm going to protect you. You get that, don't you?"

Then she heard an engine gunning. A truck horn blared. Then with a horrific screech the truck flew through the front window.

Eric bellowed in anger and charged toward the truck, gun firing. But it was too late. Joshua leaped from the door. He rolled, took Eric out at the knees and dropped him to the floor. Eric thrashed against Joshua's grip. Joshua pinned him like a rag doll.

"Magpie is on the way!" Eric shouted hysterically. "When Magpie gets here, you'll be dead. You'll all be dead. All Magpie cares about is me."

His hand slipped into his pocket. Too late Samantha saw the knife flash in Eric's hand. She cried out against her gag, fighting helplessly against the rope.

"You should've let me protect Samantha!" Eric slashed the knife through the air. "I'm the only one who can protect her from Magpie!"

Joshua caught the blow with his right hand and knocked the knife from Eric's grasp. Then with the left he leveled a jab to his jaw. Eric crumpled to the floor.

Sirens blared in the distance. Police. Ambulance. Rescue was coming.

Joshua's eyes were locked on Samantha's face. He ran for her.

"Are you okay?" He knelt in front of Samantha. His hand brushed her cheek. He pulled the gag from her mouth. Then his lips brushed her face, simply, tenderly. "I'm sorry I wasn't here sooner. Are you okay? Did he hurt you?"

"No, but he hit Theresa pretty hard."

He moved around between them, and she felt his fingers on her skin as he cut their wrists free.

Theresa groaned faintly. "Joshua?"

"Hey, Theresa." He knelt beside them, his voice gentle. "Don't worry, help is on their way."

"You drove a truck into my office?" Theresa's voice was faint but strong.

"Technically it's Alex's truck." He glanced back at Samantha. "Hermes lured me to the park and two other young men jumped me there. Judging by their appearance, I'm very sure they were the same two that kidnapped you on behalf of Magpie. I'm getting the impression that Eric made people do a lot of terrible things." He glanced at Eric with disgust.

"Zoe and Alex disarmed them and are holding them until the police arrive."

Relief flooded her limbs. "The four women on Roy's list were all women Eric cared about. They all died in various suspicious ways. Eric says he hired Roy to find out who was killing these women. He's clearly unwell. I thought before he was taking some kind of methamphetamines and clearly they've done some real damage to his brain. I'm not sure if he thought he was kidnapping me to protect me from Magpie or as some kind of bait to lure Magpie out into the open."

Joshua looked down at the crumpled man on the floor. "You do realize there might have never even been a Magpie. Magpie was just a delusion Eric created to let him kill. At least now the nightmare's over."

They were safe. The people who'd kidnapped her had been arrested.

But still something still didn't feel quite right. Like there was still something, a piece still missing. Like the picture still wasn't complete.

They heard the sirens first. Then came the lights. Then came the people in uniform, swarming in, taking over. Theresa was taken to the hospital. Eric was led away in handcuffs. Police took her statement. Paramedics checked her for injuries. And through it all, Joshua never left her side, with his hand on her shoulder, or holding her fingers, or brushing her back. Until finally, they were free to walk a few steps away from the crowd and stand on the street corner, in comfortable silence together, watching as fresh snow fell. Her head fell against his shoulder.

If only I could freeze this moment forever. This one moment, feeling safe, feeling strong.

Alex materialized through the crowd, his clothes looking like he'd just fought his way through an army, but with a twinkle in his eye that said he wouldn't hesitate to do it again. "You promised not to crash my truck."

Joshua smiled and ran his hand over his jaw. "Had to be done. You understand."

"I do." He dropped a set of keys into Joshua's hands. "Zoe's with Theresa. They haven't really spoken in years, but one good thing about today is that the rift's now closed. I'm going to wait for the tow truck. You can use Zoe's car to take Samantha to the train station. Unless you're planning on driving Samantha all the way to Montreal to see her family."

Alex chuckled. But for once Joshua didn't seem ready to join in the joke.

"Thanks." Joshua frowned slightly and patted Alex on the shoulder. "I'll see you guys back at the house in time for dinner."

Alex's smile faded. "You okay?"

"I'm fine. Just don't—"

A loud buzzing sounded from her pocket. She hadn't even remembered that she still had her phone. She pulled her phone out of her pocket. It was Yvonne. "Hang on, I've got to take this."

She took a step away from the men, leaving them to continue their conversation in hushed voices, and answered the phone. "Yvonne! Hi!"

Her landlady's tone was so cold it could've chipped ice. "I'm calling to let you know that I've called a moving company to empty your apartment and put your belongings into storage. If you want to come by and pick up the key or to send somebody else by, you can. But I run a respectable building. I just can't have the kind of nonsense going on with one of my tenants that you've put me through the past twenty-four hours."

Samantha almost laughed. Two days ago the thought of losing an apartment that sweet in the middle of downtown Toronto would've been enough to put her in an overthinking tailspin. But now, after everything she'd been through, the idea of one paranoid woman who wanted to run a downtown Toronto apartment building like some boarding school was, well, laughable.

"You can't kick me out of my apartment without going through due process," she said, her voice feeling firm in her chest. "I will come right over, supervise the removal of my stuff and sign off on the storage unit, because I want my stuff to be safe and I don't have any reason to trust that you're not going to get someone to pick the lock on my new door while I'm visiting my parents for Christmas. But let me make something clear, that's still my apartment. If you want to break the lease and kick me out like this, I will take you to the landlord tenant tribunal. Not because I want to live in your building, but because you're not going to get away with treating your tenants like wayward children." Samantha could hear her spluttering, mustering up some new sob story. But Samantha had listened long enough. "Goodbye, Yvonne. See you in half an hour."

Samantha hung up the phone and stuck it in her pocket. She looked up. Alex had gone. Joshua was looking at her.

"Change of plans. Yvonne is trying to push me out of my apartment. She says she's called a moving company. I'm going over there to sort it out. Then I'll head to the station and hopefully still catch a later train. If not, there are plenty of buses."

Joshua nodded. They headed for Zoe's car. But it wasn't until he'd pulled out of the small main street and back onto the main highway that she realized she hadn't heard him speak more than a few words confirming directions. His hands gripped the steering wheel at two and ten. His eyes stared straight ahead through the windshield at the gray road.

"Look, I could tell that lame joke Alex made about driving me to Montreal hit you the wrong way," she said. "But don't worry. You've done more than enough. I'll be perfectly safe on a crowded train and my parents will meet me at the other end."

"It's okay." He still wasn't looking at her. "Although, I guess you're not needing a bodyguard anymore, now that the guys who kidnapped you have been arrested and Eric turned out to be Magpie—"

"Eric didn't turn out to be Magpie," she said quickly. "You just guessed that he was. And you might be right. But you might not."

Joshua's eyebrows rose. "I can't believe you're still defending him, after what he did to you."

"I'm not defending him! I'm just…" Her

voice trailed off. She leaned her head back against the seat. "I'm just looking at this like a fact-checker. Eric hired Roy to figure out who was behind the disappearance of Holly, Jessica, Monique and Isobel aka Bella. Why would he do that if he killed them? Why would he keep coming back to the building looking for Isobel if he'd killed her? Why would he know that Jessica and Monique were dead, but didn't know for sure that Holly and Bella were?"

Joshua rolled his eyes. "Because he probably had some kind of psychotic break when he killed his first victim, didn't want to face what he'd done, so imagined this fictional character named Magpie who solved all his problems."

"Okay," she said, "I'm willing to believe he's emotionally unstable and I wouldn't be surprised if he has some kind of substance-abuse problem. But it takes brains to invent a fictional serial killer to pin your crimes on. Magpie is a show-off. Magpie wanted to be noticed. Eric and Magpie want different things. Why would Magpie kill each of his victims in a different way? Why would Eric invite me for coffee and drop off a Christmas gift at my house the same morning he knew he'd hired two people to kill me? And how did he hire them anyway? How did he coerce them into killing people? And why do they call him Magpie?" She could see words and questions floating in her mind like jigsaw puzzles. There were still too many things that didn't click, too many things that didn't make sense.

"Evil people do evil things," Joshua said. He pulled off the highway and into the narrow roads leading to her apartment. "Our job is to stop them without asking questions. Not to try to find all the pieces and figure out why."

"Is that something else your grandfather used to say? That your job as a soldier was to follow orders, stop evil people and not think?" she said. "Because that doesn't sound like the Joshua I've met. The Joshua I know who used his brains and wits to protect me and save my life. Even if you do want to say your job isn't to question—mine is. My job is to look at the facts, figure out which ones are missing and flag those ones that don't make sense."

Joshua was silent for a long moment. Then he pulled to a stop on the street in front of her apartment. She scanned the road. No moving vans. Maybe Yvonne had relented.

"Look, some things don't make sense." He

put the car into Park. His jaw set. "And they never will."

"I don't even know what you mean by that," she said. But there was something in his tone that stung like a rebuke. "I'm sorry if it was presumptuous of me to ask you to drive me back to my apartment. I know you only agreed to keep an eye on me as a favor to Daniel and Olivia. There's no reason for you to keep escorting me around now."

She unbuckled her seat belt and pulled her bag over her shoulder.

"Look, we really do need to talk." He looked up at her building. "How about we go in, get your stuff sorted and then grab a coffee at the train station?"

"Is that what you want?" She turned to face him on the seat. "Because you've been in an odd mood ever since you talked to Alex back at the crime scene. And this isn't the first time. Yesterday, I thought you were spending time with me because you wanted to. You seemed like you wanted to. But then it was like you pushed me away and told me you were only there because Daniel had asked you to be my bodyguard. Then last night, when you plucked me from the storm you held me so tightly and kissed me. I thought it meant something. But then you pushed me away again." Frustrated tears pressed against her eyelids. Her eyes rose to the ceiling. "It's not easy for me to trust anyone, Joshua, you get that? After what happened to me back in college, trust has always been really hard for me. It's like my heart just isn't as good at knowing how to open up as other people's and my brain really struggles sometimes to understand what people mean. Some moments, you're so gentle and kind and strong, it's like I can feel my heart wanting to trust you. Then something happens and you close up again. You can't just open my heart up and then slam it shut. It's not fair to me."

Joshua turned off the car and unbuckled his seat belt. Then his hands gripped the steering wheel again. "I never met my grandmother. But I know she broke my gramps's heart, and he probably broke hers too. His job meant that he was never there for her and then one night she went out to a Christmas party without him, and got hit by a car and died. Then my dad fell for my mom, and I don't remember her much either. Dad says it was love at first sight and she was all kinds of beautiful, but then she didn't much like marriage so she left soon after having me."

"Oh, Joshua, I'm so sorry." She reached out for him. Her hand, her fingers brushed his shoulder. But it remained firm and unrelenting under her touch.

"They weren't perfect men, but they were good men. They believed in duty. They believed in helping others. They warned me not to let my heart lead me astray. Now here I am, trying to decide what my future should be and I feel like I'm being pulled in six different directions at once. I can make a good pension and an amazing difference if I stay in the military, but my heart's not in it. Giving it up to throw my lot in with this new company Daniel, Alex and Zoe are setting up tugs at something inside of me. They're my friends and my favorite people, they need me and I can do a lot of good there too. But it's risky and I don't know where it's headed. The company could fail."

He turned to face her on the seat. "But I can hardly hear my brain think anymore when I'm around you, Samantha, because I'm falling for you so hard and fast I feel like a man rushing down a Black Diamond ski slope not knowing what's going to hit him at the bottom. I'm drawn to you, like I've never been drawn to anyone before. I raced through a snowstorm to save you. I threw my body on a land mine to save you. I fought three men at once and crashed a truck through a window."

He reached for her. His hand grabbed hers. His eyes focused on her face, begging her to listen. "If Gramps and Dad taught me anything about relationships it's that sometimes when feelings hit hard like this they just don't last. I don't want to hurt you. I don't want to make you promises I can't keep. So, I've got no choice but to walk away from you and take some distance. A lot of distance. Long enough to figure out if what I feel is real. I've got to say goodbye to you and walk away."

FIFTEEN

She pulled her hand back. Angry tears were forming behind her eyes and for once she didn't try to stop him from seeing them fall.

"If you want to walk out of my life because you don't want to be in my life, then go." She could feel him reach for her hand again, but she didn't let him take it. "But don't say you're going to preemptively break my heart for my own protection. You say you can't be in my life because you don't want to throw yourself headlong into something reckless and foolish? What makes you think for one moment that I want that either?"

She reached for the door handle and was about to leap out. But something made her stop. She turned back.

"I can't imagine what it was like to grow up in your home. Sounds like your grandfather and father did the best they could. But see, my parents are very happily married and have been for over thirty years. They taught me brains and hearts were supposed to work together, along with faith. They raised me to believe in love that was built slowly, with truth and respect, and proved itself to be real. Not the stupid, reckless, selfish kind some people leap into. I'm really sorry that's not the kind of love in your family tree. In a way, it's very noble of you to want to protect me from being hurt from rushing into something too fast and reckless, that's not going to work and just end up hurting us both. But if you really were falling for me, like you say you are, you'd know me well enough to know I'm not that kind of woman."

She could feel his fingers slip over the back of her hand again. Slowly this time and gently. She looked down at their hands.

"But we only met yesterday. I guess it's too much to expect that you'd actually know me." She pulled her hand out of his. "I'm going to go into my apartment and find Yvonne. Then I'm going to call a taxi to take me to the train station. If you want to check out my apartment to make sure I'm safe or talk to the taxi company yourself to make sure they're legit, that's fine. You promised Daniel you'd make sure I made it to my train safely. But after that, I think you're right. We should go our separate ways. Because if your goal is to protect my heart from falling for you, it's too late."

She leaped out of the car and closed the door behind her. He followed. He didn't speak. Neither did she. They walked up the stairs in her building in silence and looked around her apartment, then they walked back onto the landing.

"I'm going to call Daniel," Joshua said, "and ask if he, Alex or Zoe will drive you to the train station. You'll be safer with them than a taxi. Clearly, I let my emotions get out of hand, and I'm sorry for that. But the situation we've been in has been extreme and it's hard for anyone to know what they're actually feeling. Maybe, in a few months, we can try this again, as friends, when whatever this is between us has died down."

But what if what I feel for you never goes away? What if you're not just the first man able to ever reach inside my heart, you're the only one? What if what I'm beginning to feel for you, and what you're beginning to feel for me is real and we're both just too scared to see where it leads?

"That makes a lot of sense," she said. "Thank you."

"Okay, give me a moment." Joshua walked

down the stairs to the second-floor landing. She could hear him dialing. She stood on the landing and gripped the banister. So, this was what it had come to. She'd opened her heart to someone and he'd decided he didn't want it.

At least I'm not the one running away this time.

"Samantha? Is that you?"

"Yvonne?" She glanced around. "Where are you?"

"I'm in the empty apartment." Yvonne's voice was weak. "I'm sorry, but I'm kind of stuck and I need your help."

"Sure, hang on." She crossed the landing. The apartment door was ajar. She should've known Yvonne would go from threatening to evict her to calling her for help. "You know, you shouldn't be doing renovations on your own. You really should call some professional help."

She pushed the door open and stepped into the dark, spacious apartment. The smell of stale cigarettes filled her lungs. She paused. She'd done this the other day. She remembered it now. She'd been halfway to work, realized she was missing her gloves and so had come back for them. She'd just been trying to get back into her apartment when she'd heard Yvonne calling her. She hadn't been able to see a thing. But she'd smelled something. The stench of cigarettes. She'd heard a voice wheezing. And another voice saying, *That's the one. Take her.*

The door swung shut behind her. She still couldn't see much of anything. Just empty boxes and rags. "Yvonne? Where are you?"

"I'm in here, dear. In the kitchen."

She walked around the corner and she saw Yvonne. Her landlady was sitting perfectly still on a wooden chair, with her hands behind her back. A canister full of black powder sat on her lap. A young man stood behind her, with a scar that cut across his face and a stench of old cigars. With one hand he pressed a gun to her temple, with the other he held down the button of a detonator switch.

"Help me." Yvonne's voice quivered. Her tinted glasses lay broken on the floor. "He broke in here looking for you. He's got me holding some kind of explosive. He told me he'd kill me if I didn't lure you here."

Samantha stared into the scarred face of the man who'd tied her up, who'd kidnapped her and shoved a land mine under her back. He smirked. She held her ground and didn't look away. "What do you want?"

"It's not me," he said. The snarl in his voice

wavered. "Magpie wants you. You come with me to see Magpie. He'll let Yvonne live."

"I'm so sorry, Samantha." Long white-blond hair streamed down Yvonne's face. Bright blue eyes looked up into Samantha's, full of tears. "Please, do wherever he wants. Or he'll kill me."

And suddenly, Samantha could feel the puzzle pieces that had been floating around in her mind suddenly, irrevocably, click into place.

She finally knew who Magpie was. She finally knew what Magpie wanted.

But this time Joshua wasn't here to save her.

He'd dialed, the phone was ringing, but it hadn't been answered yet. Joshua closed his eyes, leaned against the wall of the second-floor landing and prayed. "God, why do I feel like I'm making the biggest mistake of my life?"

Samantha was amazing. She was everything he could ever want for in a best friend and a beloved rolled into one. And yet—

"Hello?"

"Hey, Dad?" Joshua opened his eyes.

"Hey, Josh. What's up?"

"There's something I've been wanting to

tell you, but I didn't want to disappoint you and I didn't want it to ruin Christmas."

"Okay?"

"I don't want to reenlist in the army. I'm thinking of going into private security instead."

"Uh-huh."

He closed his eyes again. "I've also met a woman. She's pretty spectacular, but I know you and Gramps used to warn me against rushing into things. I don't want anyone's heart to get broken."

"All hearts get broken. They don't always stay broken. I get off work at eight tomorrow. If you get to the house before me, feed the dog. He'll have been home alone all day."

Joshua smiled. "No problem."

"You're a smart man. Don't worry yourself into trouble. See you tomorrow."

The phone clicked off. Joshua started back up the stairs. Samantha was no longer on the landing. He knocked on her door. It swung open under his touch. Her apartment was empty.

"Hey, Samantha?"

Then a muffled scream seemed to filter through the walls. Samantha was screaming his name. He ran back onto the landing and burst through the door of Bella's empty apartment. "Samantha? Where are you?"

"In here!"

He ran for the kitchen. His eyes took in the scene.

Samantha's landlady sat on a chair in the kitchen with a black canister of powder on her lap and tears streaming down her cheeks. The young man who'd gotten away after the attack at the bridge was pressing a gun to her head with one hand and holding down a detonator with the other. A bare bulb hung from the ceiling, swinging back and forth sending shadows over the grim, gross apartment.

The picture couldn't be clearer. A man with a gun. A woman in danger.

"Please," Yvonne said. "Don't let him hurt me."

Yet, there stood Samantha, one step inside the door. Her hands were raised. But the look in her eyes was fierce, keen, almost angry. Like she could see something he didn't see. Like she'd locked onto the missing piece of the puzzle.

"Magpie sent me." The scarred man smirked. "You let me take Samantha to him, or this building explodes and everyone dies."

"You're the soldier, right?" Yvonne's eyes met his, pleading, wide. "The bodyguard?

Help me, please. This man just broke in looking for Samantha. He says he was sent by some evil master criminal named Magpie and he's threatening to kill me if she doesn't leave with him."

"Yvonne, don't worry." Joshua felt his fists raise, ready for the fight. "I'll save you and I won't let Magpie take Samantha."

"Yvonne doesn't need saving." Samantha's voice cut through the air like a knife. "And that man wasn't about to take me to Magpie."

"Please." Yvonne's head shook. "She doesn't know what she's talking about. That man is holding down the button on a detonator. If he lets go, we all die."

"Joshua." Samantha's voice dropped, until it was as calm and steady as any he'd ever followed into battle. "Trust me. The gun is real, the danger is real and if I leave with that man, I will most definitely die. But he won't take me to Magpie and I'm almost certain that impressive-looking can of black powder sitting on Yvonne's lap won't do a thing when that man lets go of that button. You were absolutely right when you said Magpie was an invention. But it wasn't Eric who invented it. Magpie is Yvonne."

"What?" No, that didn't make sense. Samantha's paranoid, fussy landlady was a serial killer who'd arranged the deaths of four women and tried to have at least another two people killed?

"She's crazy." Yvonne's voice rose. "You can't believe her. I'm not whatever she thinks I am."

"Listen to me, Joshua," Samantha said. Confidence rang in her voice. "Yvonne is Magpie. Yvonne is Eric's secret guardian who protected him by killing off the women in his life who don't love him as well as she thinks they should. Think about it. It fits. It's the only theory that fits. Yvonne used to work with youth who'd been in trouble with the law. Now she's been using them, manipulating them into killing for her. Maybe out of loyalty or some kind of blackmail, I don't know, but she admitted to me that she used to read their confidential files. Yvonne has to be Magpie. Who else has enough access to my apartment to know how to invent some perfect fictional criminal based on the very things I'd been researching? Who else could've wiped my computer? Or given those criminals the information they needed to find me, break into my work and track my movements? Why else would she harass and threaten strange visitors to the building, while practically encouraging Eric to come and go as he wanted, while pressuring me to date him?"

"Enough talk." The scarred man pressed the gun deeper into her temple. "I was sent for the girlie. I'm not leaving without her."

"Joshua, please." Yvonne's voice shook. "Convince him to let me go. It's Samantha he wants, not me. She's grasping at straws. She's the one who went for counseling today because her memory was faulty! Her memory isn't working right!"

"How did you know I was going to see a counselor today or that I was having memory gaps if you hadn't been spying or eavesdropping on yesterday's conversation?" Samantha stepped forward. A smile crossed her lips. "But you know where you slipped up most of all? The message you wrote on the hand grenade. Delete my ATHENA database. All this time, I couldn't figure out why the Magpie would want my newspaper to delete the very database I created and erase everything I work on? Until it hit me. You're the only one who had a problem with the work I do. You kept telling me that I work too much and should quit my job because it was getting in the way of my being with Eric. Then when you realized Joshua was the threat and my feelings for him could be the real problem,

Magpie's tune suddenly changed, the warnings stopped and you just sent your goons to kill him.

"See, it never made sense to couple threats with the deadly weapons like that. Unless Magpie was someone who didn't care if I died or if I ran into Eric's arms. Either one worked for you. As long as you gave your son what he wanted."

Samantha reached back and brushed Joshua's hands.

"Yvonne, the Magpie, is Eric's mother. They have the same bright blue eyes. I never noticed until now because she always hid hers behind those tinted glasses. But the stories of their pasts match up. He's the ungrateful son who never appreciates all she does for him. She's the unstable mother he had to distance himself from for the sake of his career. It even explains why he's been hanging around the building so much. She's been killing for him, probably all his life, and using other people to do it for her. And it's making him crazy."

Yvonne's eyes closed. "She's lying. She's crazy. She has no idea what she's talking about. You can't trust Samantha! She's lost her mind."

The man with the scar swung the barrel of the gun toward Joshua. "I'm counting backward from ten. You better push your girlie over to me and walk away by the time I get to one, or everyone dies."

"Joshua!" Samantha's voice rose. "Please! The bomb isn't real. The design is wrong. The detonator isn't even connected properly. Yvonne's not really in danger."

"Ten!"

I either trust Samantha. Or I don't.

"Nine!"

He didn't need eight more seconds to decide what to do.

"Samantha, get out of here! Call the police!"

Joshua charged the gunman. The weapon fired. The bullet flew into the ceiling. Joshua knocked the gunman to the ground before he could fire again. A strong blow to the head and the scarred man crumpled. He yanked the gun from his hands.

"Thank you!" Yvonne scrambled to her feet and ran toward Samantha.

"Stop!" Joshua raised the gun. "Hands on your head, Yvonne. Get down on the ground. Don't you dare take one more step toward Samantha. I might not have a brain as quick as hers and can't get my head around all the facts that make up the big picture Samantha sees which proves you're the Magpie. But I trust her, one hundred percent. So, if she's convinced you're the killer mastermind behind all this, that's good enough for me."

Yvonne paused, for a long moment. Then her hands slid deep into the canister and pulled out a gun.

"I knew I shouldn't have underestimated you." She aimed the gun at Samantha's face. "All those brains. All that tap, tap, tapping. But so blind to how much my Eric cared for you. How he would've done anything for you. I warned you to quit your job. I told his idiotic detective buddy where to find you, knowing he'd blab it to Eric, and got my boys to get Joshua out of the way to give you one last chance. I showed you mercy. That was wrong. I should've killed you the first time I knew you were going to hurt my boy." She snarled. "But first, I'm going to kill the man you do care about."

Yvonne spun toward Joshua. She fired. He dove and rolled away as the bullet tore a hole through the floor. Samantha leaped, jumping on Yvonne's back. She yanked the gun from the woman's hand and forced the Magpie to the ground.

Thank You, God! Prayer exploded like a firework in Joshua's heart.

Then he looked down to where Samantha knelt, pinning Yvonne to the floor.

Joshua swallowed hard. "Nicely done."

"Thank you. I learned by watching the best." Her eyes ran from the crumpled form of the scarred man in the corner of the room to her landlady now pinned beneath her knees. "Can you take it from here? That's the only move I really have."

He chuckled. A lump formed in his throat. "I reckon that's the only move you needed."

They sat, side by side on her couch, long after the police had come and arrested Yvonne and her thug, just staring at the twinkling lights of the Christmas tree in silence. Samantha's foul-smelling kidnapper had been quick to blurt out everything to the police when he'd come to, explaining that Yvonne had been blackmailing them into killing for her. Police confirmed that Hermes, Eric and the third youth who'd attacked Joshua at the bridge had all been arrested. Hopefully they'd be as quick to turn on the Magpie too, and get the help they needed to turn their lives around.

Joshua's hand slid into Samantha's. She squeezed his hand tightly.

"You believed me," she said. "When the

crisis hit, you trusted me over what your eyes were telling you. Even if you walk out of my life right now, I'm always going to be thankful to know somebody believed in me like that."

"I did and I do." His other arm slid around her shoulder. Her head fell into the crook of his neck. He took a deep breath and breathed her in. "You were right. You were right this whole time, and I needed to trust you."

The clock on the wall chimed softly. He looked up. It was almost two in the afternoon.

"I have to go." She pulled away, out of his arms. "If I don't head to the train station now, I won't make it to Montreal tonight." She turned toward him. "I don't want to leave you. Not like this. But you're right. I can't just throw all my plans out the window, cancel Christmas Eve dinner with my parents and rearrange my whole life for someone I just met yesterday. It's too soon to know what we feel or what happens next."

"Then how about this." He slipped off the couch and onto the floor. He knelt before her. One hand took hers, and he raised it to his mouth, feeling the softness of her skin against his lips. "Samantha Colt, I can honestly say I don't know where my life is headed. I don't think I'm going to reenlist, but I still have several more months before my term is up. I think I'm going to ask Daniel if there's a role for me in his new private security company, but I don't know what that's going to look like yet. But I can make you a promise, and I intend to keep it. I promise I will always be honest with you. I promise I will do everything in my power not to hurt you. I promise I will work as hard as I can to stay in your life, get to know you better and build this relationship into being the best possible thing it can be. Because you're beautiful, extraordinary, brave and wise, and I've never met anyone like you. I think I'm falling in love with you. So I'll do my best to be worthy of you and prove this thing between us is real, whatever the future holds. If that's what you want too. Is it?"

A beautiful smile lit up her face, sending lights dancing in the tears of joy glistening in her eyes. "Yeah, it is. I really do."

Then his hands slid up along her neck and into her hair, and he kissed her slowly. A gentle kiss. Growing stronger by the moment. A kiss that held the promise of all the moments, days and months to come.

EPILOGUE

A door slammed. Samantha woke up, her heart pounding hard in her chest. She was lying on a couch she didn't recognize. Darkness filled her eyes. The brush of waves on a sandy shore filled her ears. Warm summer breeze danced through the windows. Where was she?

Then she felt warm, strong arms sliding around her in the darkness.

"Sorry, I didn't mean to wake you. A breeze caught the door." Joshua's voice brushed against her ear. His lips brushed her cheek. "It was a long, tiring day. You fell asleep on the couch while I was bringing the bags in."

He lifted her up into his arms. The long lace train of her vintage lace wedding gown spun around her legs, then he sat down on the couch, cradling her to his chest. Her hand slipped into his. Their fingers linked and she felt the unfamiliar coolness of their wedding bands sitting side by side in the darkness.

Husband and wife. The clock chimed eleven. *It was still her wedding day.*

Had it really all happened today? Waking up in the morning in Zoe's apartment, before the summer sun had even risen? Walking down the aisle at the downtown church to slide her hand into that of the man she loved?

The man who'd patiently wooed her for months, as the love that had sparked in their hearts on the frozen morning they'd met, slowly grew into a flame, strong and secure enough to dedicate their lives to. Then the drive to the country house, home base of Joshua's employer Ash Private Security, for a wedding reception with friends, family and colleagues. Then finally, they'd driven up to the quiet, secluded cottage on the beach.

One long, incredible day, where everything in her life had changed.

She leaned back, secure in the strength of his arms, feeling his heart beating against her. He'd pulled off his jacket and bow tie on the drive to the beach. Now she could feel his white button-up shirt, open at the neck, and the softness of his arms where he'd rolled it up over his elbows.

"You falling asleep on me again?" he asked.

"Not quite yet."

"Come on, then." He swept her up into his arms again and carried her out to the beach. Warm summer breeze danced across her skin, tossing her hair around her face. Water rushed up to the shore. She looked up and saw hundreds of dazzling specks of light dancing in the darkness above her. He spun her around. She laughed. Then he set her back down in the darkness. Her bare feet sank into the sand.

"I'm sorry we couldn't have a longer honeymoon," Joshua said. "But Daniel's still setting up the business and you've got that big article you're coauthoring with Theresa about creating safer college campuses—"

"No work talk. Not right now." She put her arms around him. Her lips brushed his neck. "I'm happy. Right here, with you, and that's enough for today."

"Then how about this." Joshua's arms slid around her waist. "Samantha, my friend, my love, my wife. You're the most amazing thing that ever fell into my life and I can't imagine wanting to live a day of it without you."

She tilted her head toward him. "You won't have to."

"Thank You, God, for that."

Then he pulled her closer into his arms,

and his lips found hers in a long, passionate kiss as he held her to him tightly under the dark night sky.

* * * * *

If you enjoyed
KIDNAPPED AT CHRISTMAS,
look for these Maggie K. Black stories
from Love Inspired Suspense:

KILLER ASSIGNMENT
DEADLINE
SILENT HUNTER
HEADLINE: MURDER
CHRISTMAS BLACKOUT
TACTICAL RESCUE

Dear Reader,

Have you started your Christmas shopping yet? Maybe that's an odd question, considering the holidays might still be months away when you read this. But I'm the kind of person who shops for Christmas all year round. If I see the perfect present in February, I buy it on the spot and then save it in the top of my cupboard. Then, on Christmas Eve, I unpack it all and suddenly find extra presents I bought that I had forgotten about. (The only time this backfires is when I try to buy books for my bookworm daughter and then discover she's read them all!)

Right now, Christmas is two weeks away for me. My shopping has been finished since November. But still I'm worried—have I done enough? Right now the television is bombarding me with advertisements telling me to buy more, do more, be more. Sometimes it's hard to believe I've done enough.

I like Samantha Colt and Joshua Rhodes because they both, in different ways, struggled with doubting themselves. Yet, at the same time God is doing so much in their lives and they have a lot to look forward to as they start this amazing new life together.

Thank you for sharing their story with me. I hope that as you face the days, months and years ahead, you will find the peace, joy and strength for whatever your future holds.

As always, you can find me online at www.maggiekblack.com or on Twitter at @maggiekblack.

Merry Christmas and thank you for sharing the journey,
Maggie

LARGER-PRINT BOOKS!

GET 2 FREE
LARGER-PRINT NOVELS
PLUS 2 FREE
MYSTERY GIFTS

Love Inspired®

SUSPENSE
RIVETING INSPIRATIONAL ROMANCE

Larger-print novels are now available...

LISLP15

REQUEST YOUR FREE BOOKS!
2 FREE WHOLESOME ROMANCE NOVELS
IN LARGER PRINT
PLUS 2
FREE
MYSTERY GIFTS

⚜⚜⚜⚜⚜⚜⚜⚜⚜⚜⚜⚜⚜⚜⚜⚜⚜⚜⚜⚜⚜⚜

HEARTWARMING™

✳✳✳✳✳✳✳✳✳✳✳✳✳✳✳✳✳✳✳✳✳✳✳

Wholesome, tender romances

YES! Please send me 2 FREE Harlequin® Heartwarming Larger-Print novels and my 2 FREE mystery gifts (gifts worth about $10). After receiving them, if I don't wish to receive any more books, I can return the shipping statement marked "cancel." If I don't cancel, I will receive 4 brand-new larger-print novels every month and be billed just $5.24 per book in the U.S. or $5.99 per book in Canada. That's a savings of at least 19% off the cover price. It's quite a bargain! Shipping and handling is just 50¢ per book in the U.S. and 75¢ per book in Canada.* I understand that accepting the 2 free books and gifts places me under no obligation to buy anything. I can always return a shipment and cancel at any time. Even if I never buy another book, the two free books and gifts are mine to keep forever.

161/361 IDN GHX2

Name _____ (PLEASE PRINT) _____

Address _____ Apt. # _____

City _____ State/Prov. _____ Zip/Postal Code _____

Signature (if under 18, a parent or guardian must sign) _____

Mail to the **Reader Service:**
IN U.S.A.: P.O. Box 1867, Buffalo, NY 14240-1867
IN CANADA: P.O. Box 609, Fort Erie, Ontario L2A 5X3

* Terms and prices subject to change without notice. Prices do not include applicable taxes. Sales tax applicable in N.Y. Canadian residents will be charged applicable taxes. Offer not valid in Quebec. This offer is limited to one order per household. Not valid for current subscribers to Harlequin Heartwarming larger-print books. All orders subject to credit approval. Credit or debit balances in a customer's account(s) may be offset by any other outstanding balance owed by or to the customer. Please allow 4 to 6 weeks for delivery. Offer available while quantities last.

Your Privacy—The Reader Service is committed to protecting your privacy. Our Privacy Policy is available online at www.ReaderService.com or upon request from the Reader Service.

We make a portion of our mailing list available to reputable third parties that offer products we believe may interest you. If you prefer that we not exchange your name with third parties, or if you wish to clarify or modify your communication preferences, please visit us at www.ReaderService.com/consumerschoice or write to us at Reader Service Preference Service, P.O. Box 9062, Buffalo, NY 14240-9062. Include your complete name and address.

HW15

WESTERN WP PROMISES

YES! Please send me **The Western Promises Collection** in Larger Print. This collection begins with 3 FREE books and 2 FREE gifts (gifts valued at approx. $14.00 retail) in the first shipment, along with the other first 4 books from the collection! If I do not cancel, I will receive 8 monthly shipments until I have the entire 51-book Western Promises collection. I will receive 2 or 3 FREE books in each shipment and I will pay just $4.99 US/ $5.89 CDN for each of the other four books in each shipment, plus $2.99 for shipping and handling per shipment. *If I decide to keep the entire collection, I'll have paid for only 32 books, because 19 books are FREE! I understand that accepting the 3 free books and gifts places me under no obligation to buy anything. I can always return a shipment and cancel at any time. My free books and gifts are mine to keep no matter what I decide.

272 HCN 3070 472 HCN 3070

Name	(PLEASE PRINT)

Address	Apt. #

City	State/Prov.	Zip/Postal Code

Signature (if under 18, a parent or guardian must sign)

Mail to the **Reader Service:**
IN U.S.A.: P.O. Box 1867, Buffalo, NY 14240-1867
IN CANADA: P.O. Box 609, Fort Erie, Ontario L2A 5X3

READERSERVICE.COM

Manage your account online!

- Review your order history
- Manage your payments
- Update your address

> ### We've designed the Reader Service website just for you.

Enjoy all the features!

- Discover new series available to you, and read excerpts from any series.
- Respond to mailings and special monthly offers.
- Connect with favorite authors at the blog.
- Browse the Bonus Bucks catalog and online-only exculsives.
- Share your feedback.

Visit us at:

ReaderService.com